BILLIONAIRE BOSS

A SECRET BABY ROMANCE

NATASHA L. BLACK

COPYRIGHT

Copyright © 2020 by Natasha L. Black

1

―――――――

CAT

The building was even more imposing than I remembered from my days as an intern. Somehow it hadn't seemed so gleaming and intimidating then. I guess because I was still in school at the time. It had seemed like a game, like playing at having a corporate job. My livelihood hadn't depended on it. I had student loans and a work-study job for that. Now it was me and my degree, all alone against the accruing interest on my loan payments.

I wore a black pantsuit from the mall and a pair of slightly used designer boots off eBay, and I was ready for day one at my new job in HR at Astley Corp. I shook my hair, tried to pretend I had a Kate Middleton style blowout instead of just the best my flat iron could do at home.

At the reception desk I got my picture taken for my ID badge so I could access the upper floors. Security searched my bag, and I went through the metal detector. Once I had an elevator key fob, I went up to the thirty-sixth floor where Kim greeted me.

She had been my mentor when I interned, so having her

for a supervisor was like a dream. I already knew and trusted her, and I was thrilled that she had enough faith in me to hire me as part of her team. I wanted to impress her and prove myself. I stuck out my hand to shake hers, but she greeted me with a hug.

"Welcome back, Cat. I'm glad you've come on board."

"I loved it here when I interned. I didn't think you'd have room in HR for me with the staff you already had."

"Ben had to be let go. And you were my first choice to replace him. Now let's get you settled, and I'll introduce you to the major players. You'll even meet Holly, the new intern," she said.

Too bad for Ben, I thought to myself as I followed behind Kim. I put my stuff down at the desk she gave me and said hi to everyone. I knew them all except Holly, who seemed tentative and nervous—I wondered if I had been that way at first, too. I made a mental note to be extra patient with her.

The floor HR occupied was all black and chrome, sleek and shining as the building itself, but decorated with motivational posters meant to boost office morale. Kim took me over to the finance department and then up to legal and introduced me to the supervisors and a few people our department worked closely with. Everyone was friendly and welcoming. Then she took me up to the executive suite —the top two floors reserved for the ruling class, the chiefs with their assistants and the head legal counsel, as well as office space for the board of directors when they needed it.

The executive floors were warmer and fancier in décor. The tile floors were replaced with a plush carpet woven in a pattern that looked Turkish. Our footsteps were muted by the plush pile. Everything that was shiny on the main floors was a burnished gleam here—with deep wood paneling and tasteful, yet expensive wallpaper figured in navy blue and gold. It made me think of French kings, of monarchs and rulers, and of a hushed reverence of a palace. I met Marie, the CFO, whose credentials had impressed me and whose demeanor was all business.

The Chief Operating Officer was on a call, but I met his assistant, a very handsome blond man named Chris, who promptly showed me pictures of his husband and their dogs. I liked him instantly and hoped we could have lunch sometime.

I was nervous about meeting the CEO himself because everyone knew that Brent Waltham was a self-made man, brilliant and hard-working. I had saved the copy of Forbes with him on the cover. He looked like a stern, sexier George Clooney. I'd be lying if I said all I'd done was read the articles. In pictures I'd seen him in, he was portrayed as a business role model who was both mouth-wateringly sexy and intimidating. I would be so mad at Photoshop if he turned out to be five feet tall and an absolute troll. As it was, I could conjure up the image of that Forbes cover, his face partly in shadow, a serious, pensive expression on his chiseled features, the smirk of his full lips enough to make me melt inside. I swallowed hard just thinking of that picture.

I will not make a fool of myself over the boss.

I will not get nervous and babble. I am qualified and capable with every right to be here.

I will not stand here and cream my panties overseeing his brass nameplate.

A framed huge picture of the board of directors with Brent Waltham hung on the wall. With his stern, square jaw, piercing dark eyes, and fuck-me mouth. What would I say when I met him? *Hi, I'm Cat Sherman, the new HR assistant. Please say my name nice and slow, so I can remember it when I fantasize at night about this later.*

Mr. Waltham's assistant, Millie, a nice older woman, said he wasn't in a meeting and buzzed to see if he could see us. She sent us right in. I fidgeted and put my hands in my pockets only to realize I couldn't shake his hand if I had my hands in my pockets.

"Mr. Waltham, good morning. Thanks for taking the time to see us. I wanted to introduce you to Cat Sherman, the new HR assistant," Kim said.

"It's an honor to meet you, sir," I said solemnly, shaking his hand.

His hand was big and warm, the palms rougher than I expected. He gripped my hand firmly but not too hard, not like a man with anything to prove, and then released it.

"That's how you know you're getting old, Kim. When the new hires call you sir," he said with a powerhouse grin that made my feet tingle inside my eBay shoes.

"I didn't mean—" I began, then I stopped, "It was a honorific," I said.

"So you say," he said, "But I am probably twice your age, Ms. Sherman."

"And with the accomplishments to prove it, Mr. Waltham," I said smoothly.

"Well done. Kim, are you sure she shouldn't be in PR? She handled that with remarkable confidence."

"Thanks," I said before Kim could answer, "Kim was my mentor when I interned here. So if I acquitted myself well at all, it's what she's taught me."

"Again, a masterful response. She attributes the credit to you, Kim. I think she could be a successful political spokesperson—or a confident man."

Again he addressed Kim and not me. He was talking about me to her. Like I was the child in the room while they were adults. It annoyed me a little, but I wasn't about to show it.

"Thank you for taking the time to meet me. I doubt our paths will cross very much, but I'm a great admirer of your work, particularly your dedication to green solutions in business. Your environmental best practices were taught in my graduate program."

"That's it, I ought to be in a nursing home. They're teaching about me in colleges now like I'm Charles Dickens two hundred years dead," he said with a wry laugh.

The man didn't look a day over forty, although I knew that he was forty-seven or would be soon. Not quite twice my age but near enough. He had the confidence to laugh about his age, which was dead sexy as well. His low, rumbling voice and big hands were more of an aphrodisiac than oysters and champagne on a beach at sunset.

It felt as though my whole body had some kind of uncontrollable reaction to him. His physical presence after two years of fantasizing about him was potent. Ugh, why did I keep thinking of sex words like potent and aphrodisiac? I was not a fourteen-year-old boy, and there was no reason to have sex on the brain. On my first day at work. In an office with my actual boss and her actual boss.

"Thank you, Brent," Kim said with a smile, totally oblivious to my internal meltdown. Speaking of melting, I was sweating. I had armpit sweat and my hairline was getting damp. My body was trying to lure him with pheromones or something. I wanted to laugh because it was so ridiculous that I was trying to appear cool and professional while my body wanted to fire on all cylinders. I nodded to Mr. Waltham and headed out the door.

"Please, join us at the board meeting tomorrow. You'll gain a lot of insight into how things are done. It's like a window to the inner workings of the company, and you'll meet some real heavy hitters. Some of the most philanthropic and forward-thinking men and women of our time sit on this board. They put my poor efforts to shame, I can tell you," he said.

"We'd love to, thanks," Kim said, answering for us both. I was glad to get into the elevator.

"Is he always like that?" I said.

"Acting like he's offended about his age? No. He does have a rather dry sense of humor, but you'll get used to it. He's a fair man, and intelligent beyond anything I can describe. You can be proud to work for him," she said almost reverently. "You seemed nervous in there."

"I was. I mean, the guy's a legend, Kim. He's been on magazines, and he accepted the James Award for Environmentally Conscious Business last year—it was televised from Lincoln Center."

"You watched that?" she said.

"Didn't everyone?"

She chuckled. "I don't think everyone watched it, no. The fact that you did makes me think you're either extremely dedicated to your work, or else you're a corporate fangirl."

"Can I claim both? Because I will admit I've followed his career."

"But when I offered to introduce you last summer, you turned me down."

"I was wearing a flowered sundress. I was too nervous about meeting him and I looked like a refugee from the set of Little House on the Prairie in the 1970s."

Kim laughed, "I think you and he would get along fine. You sound like him."

"I bet he'd look pretty good in a sundress," I quipped.

"Very funny. Now let's get you to work."

I spent the afternoon getting up to speed on updated policies and the procedures for annual appraisals and for employee improvement plans. I was put to work on refining the remediation recommendations for employee absences with Heather, a woman I'd worked with before. She was informative and the work was interesting, which made the day fly by.

As soon as work was over, I texted my friends back home to let them know that day one was a success and that my boss was super-hot.

Maddie replied first. *I think ur allowed to sleep with him as long as you don't harass him about it.*

But Sarah Jo said it was unethical to sleep with the boss. To which Layla replied, *shut up ur still in college u have guys in the dorms to sleep with whenever u want.*

I laughed myself silly over the exchange, but I knew there was no real chance I'd be personally involved with the famed CEO of Astley Corp. The most I could do was log a stellar job performance for my own HR record and catch the occasional glimpse of him in a meeting or coming out of an elevator. He was exactly that rare, Clooney brand of dashing handsomeness, the sort that came with a perpetual bronze glow to the skin and an effortless charm designed to make women drop their panties instantly.

I was tired that night and went to bed early, but I woke the next morning energized and excited about the board meeting. I wore my dress—the navy blue sheath I'd bought at a consignment shop. It fit perfectly, and with my taupe shoes, it looked really sophisticated. I had some tiny pearl studs that had been my grandma's, so I wore those. I twisted my hair back and pinned it into a low ballet bun at the nape of my neck. I felt like Grace Kelly. If Grace Kelly had had dark hair and been ten pounds overweight from eating one too many takeout pizzas and not doing enough yoga during grad school.

I breezed through security and met Kim in the coffee room on the HR floor. She drank a half-caffeinated mocha, but I stuck to water because I wanted to avoid coffee breath. It wasn't like we would be playing spin the bottle in a board meeting, but I wouldn't risk it anyway.

"I'm going to take notes," I said, showing her the leather folio with my legal pad and pen in it.

"I'd be disappointed if you didn't. Although everyone else uses a tablet or a phone."

"Dare to be different, " I said.

In the conference room, I boggled a little at the length of the table—a stunning creation of renewable bamboo rather than the rain-forest-trashing mahogany that was so popular in executive suites. The room was facing west, designed to avoid glare in morning meetings, and a craft service worker was pouring juice and coffee at a drink station in reusable glassware. I was glad that the company didn't talk about environmentalism and then eat donuts on styrofoam plates like hypocrites. There were no donuts in evidence though. Only beverages and fruit. I wasn't going to sit there eating a banana and looking suggestively over it at our CEO. I nearly snorted at the thought.

The seats filled and the meeting came to order. While the secretary read the minutes of the last meeting, I snuck my phone from my handbag and texted Maddie: *he is so hot I considered making eyes at him while eating a banana* and suppressed a laugh when she replied, *do it, deep throat that banana. You'll make an impression for sure.*

"Miss Sherman, was it?" Brent Waltham said.

My eyes snapped to his and my face flushed.

"I realize you're of a younger generation, but in my day when you were caught passing notes, you had to read them to the whole class."

2

———

BRENT

At first, I was irritated. I'd given the girl the opportunity to sit in on a board meeting. It was quite an honor. And she had the audacity to play on her phone while Marian read the minutes of the last meeting

I called her out on it. I didn't get to my level of success by indulging people who lacked decorum and dedication.

"I apologize, Mr. Waltham. I shouldn't have had my phone out, you're right. I was texting a friend back home, ironically, about how exciting it was to be included in the meeting. As you can see, I take the meeting seriously. I came prepared to take notes."

She held up a notepad in a folder. I frowned at it, "You brought paper?"

"Well, two reasons: one, I get in trouble when I use my phone here apparently, and two, in a nod to your advanced age, I was going old school."

I narrowly avoided laughing outright. She was so damn sassy. Her apology had seemed sincere, and the fact that she could keep up with my note passing sarcasm regarding my age made me want to raise a glass to her and make a toast.

I was stunned to feel my blood heat at her cheeky remark, to note the blush staining her cheek and her throat. I had embarrassed her, but she had given it right back to me instead of backing down, cowed by my rank. I did grant her a half-smile. She took up her pen and poised it above the paper, ready to write.

Throughout the meeting, I kept glancing at her. Her attention always rapt on the speaker or taking swift, messy notes on her legal pad. It had been a long time since a woman intrigued me so much.

I couldn't resist noticing the sweep of her elegant neck, the curve of a dark curl that had escaped its hairpins to nestle along her collarbone. I wanted to brush it back, tuck it back in its pins and put my mouth to the hollow of her throat there. I shook myself. Nowhere in Robert's Rules of Order did it list the procedure for sucking the alluring neck of a new employee. I was fairly certain that it was expressly forbidden in our corporate conduct manual.

I went to lunch with a few of the directors. One of the newer additions, a legend whose father had started on the board when the company went public years before, said he was uncomfortable with how the new hire answered me. Before I could calmly inform him that I had a sense of humor and my ego wasn't so easily bruised. Besides, the chairman, Alex Barnes, took care of it.

"Brent isn't fragile, Nate. He jokes around with his staff. He's gotten to where he is through hard work, and he doesn't demand artificial signs of respect."

"Although if you want to genuflect every time you see me, I'll allow it," I said wryly, and they all laughed.

"I still forget and kiss his ring from time to time, " Alex joked.

We talked over our role in an upcoming global conference on responsible commerce in Taiwan. Our COO was on board to attend and be the keynote speaker, which suited me perfectly. I enjoyed travel, but at this point, I was bored of delivering some version of a hopeful speech to a roomful of half-drunk executives who would have applauded just as much if I'd just stood there reciting the alphabet backward. Some of the delegates would be there because they wanted to embrace stewardship, others just wanted free drinks and accommodations on the company's dime. I was past caring about which ones were which. It'd tilted at those windmills myself a decade ago, and I had grown a bit jaded around the edges. I had no less energy, no less passion, but a hell of a lot less patience.

"Nate," I said, "your dad once told me that the way he knew he was getting old was when he stopped suffering fools. So I think I've reached that ripe old age because I'm delighted to send another executive to the conference. I won't have to stand in a buffet line for bland chicken and oversalted rice, and I won't have to listen to the same half-baked ideas in a dozen speeches."

"He never suffered fools, don't listen to him," Alex declared.

"I guess I was surprised you let her talk to you like that, but I think you were right. You're building rapport with staff and that breeds loyalty. Brand loyalty, as we know is—"

"It's not brand loyalty. It's company culture," I interrupted. "And culture is the single most important asset you have. It's where your energy belongs because a positive and compassionate culture attracts and keeps the best people. It makes them more productive and glad to be more productive. They'll do more than you ask, and they'll be grateful for the chance to do it. My grandmother used to say, you have a lot of choices to make in life, and most of them boil down to—am I going to act like a decent person or not?"

"You should give the speech in Taiwan. You're full of grandmotherly wisdom," Alex said.

"I am nobody's grandmother," I said, "and if she were here, she'd probably slap both of us up the side of the head for the way we talk. She'd call it mischief and nonsense."

"Your mischief and nonsense are worth billions," Alex countered.

"She wouldn't care. She was a terrific woman, my grandmother. In her honor, I think we should order steaks."

"Did she love steaks?" Nate said.

"I doubt she ever ate one. We didn't have that kind of money. We ate a lot of Hamburger Helper when I was growing up," I said.

"You're kidding. I knew you were self-made, but I assumed that meant you went to Yale on a scholarship instead of a family endowment."

"I went to a state school, Nate. And worked my way through. But my lack of an Ivy League pedigree hasn't held me back much. Socially, if you didn't go to Wharton, you're lesser, but being one of the 'lesser' billionaires isn't a hardship to me. I take pride in the fact that I know what it's like on both sides. I've been poor—like the electricity was shut off poor. "

"Remember the furor about ten years ago when all our employees were raised to fifteen dollars an hour minimum?" Alex said, "everyone in the industry had a fit, said we'd go bankrupt. We're still here."

"But nobody who works for me has to sleep in their car or eat ramen every night and that's a matter of pride. So teasing doesn't hurt my ego, but anyone on my payroll suffering because I was a miser—that would be a source of shame."

We drank to avoiding shame.

Speaking of shame, I couldn't help thinking that I should be ashamed of the way I'd looked at Cat Sherman, ashamed of the way I had wondered how she'd taste.

3

CAT

The next day, my third day as an Astley Corp. employee, I asked Kim if I could go apologize to the CEO in person for texting in the meeting.

"I still want to know what you were texting," she said archly.

"No. You don't. It was stupid, and I'd like a chance to tell him privately that I know it was a mistake. It won't happen again. I realize a CEO doesn't have a bunch of space in his schedule for junior staff to grovel about their mistakes, but I'd appreciate a chance if you think of anything."

"You could take him this," she said. Kim took a document off the pile on her desk, paper clipped it and put it in a folder, "here. Tell Millie I told you to hand-deliver it to him."

"Doesn't that sound like I don't trust her to give it to him?" I said.

"Look, do you want an excuse or not?" Kim asked.

"Yes, I do. Thank you. I'll be right back unless he makes me scrub the Turkish carpets for penance."

"I don't think you're even allowed to get them wet, so I doubt it. But if he has you bleach the tile grout in the bathrooms, be sure to get the part behind the toilet," she teased.

"Haha," I said flatly. I dodged into the bathroom to check my reflection and fluff my hair. I went up the elevator, the blood singing in my veins with the excitement of seeing him again.

I truly didn't want to lose my job for screwing up in the meeting, but I also wanted a chance to see him again, hear his voice, and maybe shake his hand. I bit down on my lip at the memory. Then I told myself to stop it and control my urges. Honestly, it was a pathetic crush. The fact that he was hotter than hell in person just made matters worse.

Millie had me take a seat and wait. When the massive double doors to his office opened, Brent beckoned me in. I hoped my knees would hold me. He had his jacket off and his button-down was open at the collar. He looked like he'd been running his hand through his dark hair with its sexy hint of silver. I forgot how to say words or use my hands normally as I followed him inside. The door closed behind me. I gripped the back of a chair, looked off to the side to admire the view from his palatial corner office and avoid his eyes at the same time.

"You wanted to see me?" he said.

I nodded.

"Did you need something?" he prompted.

"Oh. This. Kim wanted this hand-delivered to you. It's a document," I said lamely. I had been so excited to come to the top floor and see him that I'd neglected to ask what I was even taking to him. It could be a carryout menu from the Thai place down the street for all I knew.

He took the folder, "Are you aware of email?" he said,

"because it is no longer necessary to hand-deliver intra-office mail. We have computers for that."

"No, I know about all that. I just really like riding in elevators. Kim knows how much I love it, so she gave me an excuse."

"So my elevators are thrilling," he said with mild amusement.

"More than you know," I said, and I felt his eyes bright and mischievous on me.

His gaze raked all over me, from my face all the way down to my shoes. I felt seen, noticed, thoroughly looked at from head to toe. My pulse sped up. It was difficult to breathe when I was in the room with him. Especially when a small part of me, the part that had a teenage crush on him, wanted to grab his hands and say, *yes, you want me. I have incredible potential in the business world, but you want me all to yourself. In the bedroom.* Jesus, my subconscious trafficked in bad soap opera dialogue.

"So, what are your top three favorite elevators?" he challenged.

"Well, the Astley Corp elevator is easily in the top three. Though I'd place it at second, just after the one at Rockefeller Center."

He tapped a pen against his chin. "Hmmm. I'll have to make sure to upgrade my elevators. I can't have us being second. I don't like to lose."

After a brief moment, we both laughed. I realized that I wasn't just laughing because he was funny. I was laughing because I was happy. I couldn't remember the last time I'd felt this good, this excited and almost giddy. I got a thrill just from talking with him. It was an intellectual thrill, my mind eager to rise to the challenge. I felt like I could meet him as an equal in this conversation. It was exhilarating.

"You know, I'm glad you delivered this paperwork. Unfortunately, I have a meeting that promises to be far less entertaining. Good to see you again, Ms. Sherman," he said.

"The most fun I've ever had dropping off paperwork. Have a good day," I said.

My step was buoyed all the way to the elevator from the energy of our encounter. I started laughing in the elevator because I had ranked it as a top-three elevator in our discussion as if I had favorites of such things. I would've said anything, would've offered to compare the quality of various brands of toilet paper just to keep him talking to me. I smiled all the way back to my desk.

"So, did he accept your apology?" Kim said.

Well shit, I'd forgotten the reason I'd gone up there in the first place.

4

BRENT

Club Nine-Three was crowded that evening. It was a good thing we had a reservation. Malcolm, Tom, Drew and I were meeting for our monthly steak dinner.

The conversation was low and the tables were spaced well for privacy. The entire club was exactly the quintessential gentleman's club, complete with leather chairs and dark wood, a crackling fire in a stone fireplace that boasted a mounted stag's head above the mantle. It represented everything I had tried to attain when I started my own business—acceptance from the old boys' club, the successful elite. When I was invited to join as a member of Club Nine-Three, it felt like a major achievement, proof I'd accomplished a great deal and become a powerful man.

Looking back on it now, it was a meaningless status symbol. The exorbitant membership dues were only worthwhile because the restaurant served the best steak in three states. So we had our dinners there more often than not. Over steak and exquisitely smooth bourbon, we caught up on each other's lives and boasted of our business exploits.

These were the friends I'd made along the way.

Malcolm had helped me set up my first marketing department when I was starting out. Tom was a former VP for Astley who'd left to start his own successful PR firm, and Drew was a former intern of mine from ten years back who had become a close friend as well.

"So, this is your last dinner as a free man, eh Tom?" Drew said, sipping his drink.

"It can't come soon enough for me," Tom said.

"You think so now," I said.

"We know, you're a confirmed bachelor, Brent," Tom said.

"I wouldn't say that."

"Then what would you say?" Drew prompted.

"I'd say I like women, just not well enough to live with one," I grinned.

"Then you haven't met the right one," Tom insisted.

"I've met more than one, I assure you," I said.

"We all know you've been around," Malcolm chuckled, setting his drink down, "but I'm the only one who remembers you were married before."

"Wait, you were?" Drew said. "How did we not know that?"

"Because I don't normally talk about it."

"What was she like?" Drew said eagerly.

"She was demanding," I said plainly, "which was only part of the problem."

"And the rest of the problem was that Astley Corp is really your wife and she was only your girlfriend?" Tom said, "You were probably too young to understand the kind of commitment you were entering into. It's so fulfilling to give all of yourself to another person, to put your heart in their keeping and—"

"Good Christ Tom, save it for the wedding toast," I

chuckled. "I wish you every happiness, make no mistake. I'm a unique case, I think. A man who can enjoy the company of women without wanting to keep one forever."

"Oh, I think there's a lot of men like that, but when they're in a lower tax bracket, they're called players."

"So at my income level, we're international playboys? I'd believe that. Although I think the international playboy designation is reserved for men who want to have a woman in every major city and that doesn't interest me," I said.

"So you're looking for just one woman? *The* one?" Drew teased.

"No, I just don't want the drama of juggling affairs with multiple women. It never appealed to me from a practical standpoint, but more than that, it's disrespectful to the ladies involved."

"You'll be celibate as a monk then?" Malcolm said with a knowing grin.

"Little chance of that," I laughed. "I'm over forty, not over ninety."

"Poor Tom, you'll never have the chance to get a girl in every port. You're settling down too young," Drew teased.

"Oh, I am? And what was it you were telling me about thinking Sophia might be the one for you?" Tom challenged. Drew took a drink and didn't answer.

"Is that true?" I asked, "are both of the young bucks in our little group off the market?"

Drew shrugged, but his face admitted it was true. Malcolm clapped him on the shoulder, "Don't jump in just yet. Marriage gets better with age. I'm on my third, didn't marry her till I was nearly fifty, and it was the best decision I ever made. I chose a woman who wants the same things I want. A family, a comfortable home, a nice vacation," Malcolm said.

They laughed, and we talked about Tom's upcoming nuptials. He was unbothered by the teasing about the old ball and chain. Nothing had dimmed his enthusiasm for his bride. I was truly happy for him and wanted him to find that rare joy that came with having a true partner. I've never known it myself, but I knew enough men who had married the right woman at the right time to believe it existed for some. The rare and chosen few. I might have envied them a little, but I was a fortunate man. I had all I could have dreamed of, and to ask for more would be incredibly greedy.

But for my friends, for those dearest to me, I wished the sort of happiness a wife and family could bring. Those are not for everyone. I'd never found anyone I'd give everything up for. Not that I'd have to sacrifice anything, but I always thought that you'd have to love someone enough to be willing to give up everything for their sake. And if not, then they were just an accessory to your life, not the center of it. I regarded women too highly to keep one as a pet, as it were. Some women who lived in my house and saw me only rarely for charity functions or major social events, who had to fill her own time knowing she might go days without seeing me due to my work commitments. Plenty of women—beautiful, clever women —had assured me that they would lead such a life happy to be married to me, but I never wished such a half-hearted marriage on anyone. My first commitment was to my company, and a wife deserved better than second place in my life.

Did seeing Tom starry-eyed and besotted over his bride spark a glint of envy in me? Certainly, but no more than his youth or idealism did. There was no reason to expect him to fare better than fifty percent of marriages that end in divorce those days, but the union held such promise, and he had such hope. Was being jaded merely the wearing away of that optimism over the course of years?

In my office earlier, when Cat had brought the paperwork to me, I'd been stunned by how easily we fell into conversation. Not only conversation but banter, the sort that made Tracy and Hepburn famous, and that made me think for no reason at all of that glamorous couple's significant age difference. Bogart and Bacall. That gorgeous human rights lawyer George Clooney married. Plenty of older men found fiery young women to marry them, but I wasn't in the market for a wife or even for a lover. I had simply been attracted to the sharp back and forth of our conversation, the energy between us. She was feisty and sharp, full of fun. I wondered if I could call her up to my office to carry those papers back to Kim for me. Would it be a joke, or would it be too obvious that I wanted to see her again and talk that way, forgetting everything but the present effervescent moment?

My attention traveled back to Tom as he and Drew talked about the yacht—Malcolm's yacht—where Tom's wedding would be held. I supposed a yacht on the Adriatic Sea was picturesque and romantic. We were lucky they didn't rent a castle in Scotland or something absurd. He had bought her a lavish wedding gift, which he was describing.

"It's a sapphire necklace and earrings. The set was originally given to Wallis Simpson by Edward VIII before he abdicated. One of the greatest love stories of all time, and I'll give her a piece of it to show her what she means to me," he said.

"Beautiful. She'll love it," Malcolm said.

"I wish I'd thought of it first," Drew lamented. "Sophia loves the royal family. Maybe I can find something that belonged to Princess Diana to give her for Christmas. There isn't enough time to be sure of its provenance, though unless you go through Sotheby's..."

"Wallis Simpson was a Nazi," I informed them helpfully.

"You are such a buzzkill," Drew said. "And it won't stop me from finding a pair of earrings or something. Surely they have some availability connected to Diana now...she had tons of jewelry."

Drew promptly pulled out his phone and started looking for royal jewelry associated with a certain doomed princess. I shook my head indulgently as our steaks arrived. I cut into the thick, juicy meat, the perfect amount of red in the center, and thought that it didn't get any better than this. With a sigh of satisfaction, I tucked into my meal.

In the lull of conversation, Malcolm took out his phone and showed us a video of his son River splashing in his bath while Malcolm's wife Sophia laughed and leaned in for a selfie with their adorable, chubby baby. I nodded approval and commented that he was growing up to be as handsome as his godfather—myself. I stopped eating for a moment and took a drink of water. Something wasn't settling well with my meal perhaps. I had felt something sharp in my stomach or chest when I looked at that toddler. I'd felt it earlier when Tom was talking about his fiancée. Indigestion? If this kept up, I might have to see a doctor about a prescription antacid.

I couldn't be nauseated by the sweetness and happiness of my friends. I wasn't such a curmudgeon. I wished them the best and rejoiced in their happy families. So why did it give me a physical pang to watch that kid splashing water at his mother? It must have been too much steak sauce. Or bourbon too late at night. I shrugged it off.

My ex-wife and I weren't together very long. We were married less than two years in all. She hadn't been a bad person, and neither had I. Our faults just weren't compatible for a peaceful coexistence. She thought I was home too little, so she spent the time I was home complaining about it. I avoided home instead of trying to work out a solution that worked for us both. We didn't try counseling. I just paid off what the prenuptial agreement entitled her to, and now she sent me a Christmas card every year with pictures of her family on the ski slopes or on a white sand beach, happy and smiling. So it did work out well for someone in the end. Both of us really, because I built the company I had always wanted. And she built the family she wanted.

I just wondered what it would have been like if we had tried to stay together. If I had swallowed my pride and asked her to go to therapy with me. If we had talked it out and adjusted our expectations of each other, maybe it would have worked out. We might have had vacations and kids and been tanned and happy in our middle age together. I admit, when I got that damn card every year, I looked at her sons and her daughter and thought, for an instant, what life would be like if they had been mine. If I had taken the time to be a husband and a father. If I had someone to love, someone who loved me back.

That was where the ache came from. Not from steak sauce or bourbon or esophageal reflux. It was longing, and it tasted as bitter as hell.

Tom's wedding was bringing up all kinds of things I hadn't wanted to think about. Things I'd pushed down for years. And that coating of sadness on my tongue called to mind Cat Sherman, her lively wit and her gorgeous eyes.

She was my employee. It was unethical and off-limits entirely. Not to mention somewhat illegal.

She was also much too young. She'd be too young for Drew, about the right age for Tom. In a few years, she'd be too old for Malcolm, I thought ruefully. If he didn't stick with this current wife and the hundred thousand dollar baby, he'd probably skew even younger next time. He was tenacious, I'd give him that. He was not a man who gave up on marriage after multiple failures. He just needed a younger model to try again. Model being the operative word. I loved the guy like a brother, but sometimes you have to accept there are things you're not good at. I tried to read War and Peace in college, but I kept falling asleep so 'finishing detailed Russian novels' would be a weakness of mine. At least it didn't cost me millions in alimony to find that out. Malcolm, however, had paid more in divorce settlements than most men ever earned in a lifetime. I had rueful respect for his optimism, but I also thought it was misguided.

Tom decided to join Malcolm and me in the cigar lounge, while Drew headed home, probably to look for Princess Diana's socks on eBay. As we selected from the humidor and settled back into ample leather chairs in the quiet lounge, Tom turned to us as if we were his fathers.

"Do you have any advice for me? I mean, as I get married?" he said. "I wanted to ask you privately, so I'm glad Drew left. He'd give me hell about this. But if you have any, I don't know, *wisdom* here, lay it on me."

"Prenup. Make sure she signs one," I said, inhaling the spiced, fragrant smoke smoothly.

"Same," Malcolm admitted, "although I'd also advise you to set aside one night a month for a date night. It sounds stupid, but it's a failsafe to make sure you check in with each other. Otherwise, you can live together, share the same bed, and never know what someone's thinking or take time to really talk."

"Huh," I said sarcastically, "maybe that's where I went

wrong. We didn't schedule a date night. If I'd only had a standing reservation at Applebee's, this could all have been avoided."

"Shut up, Brent," Malcolm said, "you're the worst cynic on this subject. To listen to you, you'd think the woman took you for all you were worth and broke your heart in the bargain."

"Are you suggesting I'm more jaded than I have the right to be?"

"Perhaps," Malcolm said, drawing on his cigar.

"I love her. I want this to work. If there's any insight you can give me without being completely sarcastic, I'd appreciate it," Tom said.

I wanted to help him, but what he asked was practically a foreign language to me.

"Tom, I can tell you how to finance the acquisition of a second small company when you can't even afford the first one. I can help you decide which charities to patronize or the best ways to reduce your carbon footprint. My qualifications end there. I'm perhaps the least suited man to ask about how to make a relationship last," I said.

"Thank you for your honesty," he said soberly and turned to Malcolm.

"Malcolm doesn't know what he's talking about either. He just won't admit it as gracefully as I did," I said with a half-smile.

"Bastard," he muttered. "I know enough to ask my wife how her day was and tune in to the details. Paying attention is at least half of the battle. The rest of it is caring how she feels and what she thinks."

"So staying awake? Damn, I failed there as well," I joked.

"I'm serious. In my first two marriages, I wasn't present,

not really. My mind was the yacht I wanted to upgrade to, or the company I was looking to buy. I didn't focus on my wives as people or hold myself accountable for treating their wants and needs as priorities. And yes, the shrink that taught me that has a summer home paid for by my years in therapy after the last divorce, but the lessons I learned about communication and listening were worth every dime."

"I don't know. Did the shrink cost more than another divorce settlement? Because your ROI there may be questionable," I said.

"Don't mind Brent. He's an irreverent bastard, always has been. Likes to make a joke of everything."

"You're a good kid," I said to Tom, "and you'll do well. I have an early meeting, so I'll say good night."

"Don't let him fool you, kid," Malcolm said wryly, "all this sentiment makes him want to run for the hills."

"Fair enough," Tom said, "I can't thank the two of you enough. My brother and Drew are standing up for me, but if we'd had a larger wedding—"

"You would've made us wear matching bow ties?" I said, "I'll thank you for the thought, but I'll be going now."

"I'll order you a large in the Team Groom t-shirt," Malcolm laughed.

All the way home, I thought of Tom and the adventure he was beginning. Then my thoughts drifted back to Cat Sherman, to the sexy, hilarious way her mind worked. Something in her spirit and her smile galvanized me, woke me up from what felt like years of sleepwalking. I had opportunities, perhaps I had a future ahead of me yet that could be spent outside the office. It wouldn't be her. No one so young. No one who worked for me, but I had to give her credit for sparking the idea in me, the longing for more.

5

———————

CAT

Heather's brother was a dud. Dead boring. Like History Channel boring. Documentary about the making of toothpaste boring. I would literally commit to a two-hour YouTube viewing of paint drying if I could slip out of the restaurant unnoticed.

His name was Andy, although I nicknamed him Blandy in my head about an hour into the date. Blandy was talking about the last election. He had 'Thoughts with a capital T.' I had my own political opinions, and I took pains to research the accurate findings of any investigations in the news to avoid obviously. He didn't have the same ethic. He wanted to quote the hosts on his favorite news network, whom he referred to by their first names.

"Yeah, but isn't it all fake news?" I joked.

Blandy shook his head solemnly, "No. Not on my network. It's the only channel with the balls to tell the whole truth."

He said it totally without irony and I wondered if it was unwise to order another drink. I decided to switch to water because if I amused myself by making a drinking game of listening to him, I'd be wasted in no time. Especially if I took a drink every time he used the phrases 'seriously' and 'you wouldn't believe.'

I tried to change the subject to something I thought would be neutral.

"What's your favorite Netflix show?" I said, "Are you a Stranger Things guy? Or are you a comedy fan?"

"I don't subscribe to streaming services. They're a waste of money. I have the app on my phone so I can stay up to date with the news from the only source worth listening to. I don't watch programs or films made for entertainment. We live in troubled times, Cat. I can't believe you'd waste your brainpower on fluff like that. It's irresponsible not to devote your screen time to staying informed."

"I'm guessing you didn't watch the latest Star Wars," I said flatly.

"No. Don't tell me you did?"

"I saw it twice. And I liked it. In fact, I liked all of the Star Wars movies, even the stupid ones that came out when I was little like Phantom Menace."

"That saddens me," he said, giving me a look of grave disappointment as if I were his daughter who announced I was leaving college to join a commune or the Nazi party. I tried not to laugh.

As I ate my chicken, he made a speech about the importance of a literate and informed public rather than the reality TV consumers who think everything is a joke—possibly a dig at my sarcasm there. I took out my phone, acted like I was checking my email for work. Instead, I cued up Brent Waltham's LinkedIn profile and admired the photos. There was Brent, dashing in a tuxedo as he presented a check to a scholarship fund for the children of deceased veterans. Here was a photo of him, solemn in a gray suit and blue tie, giving a speech to the UN about responsible green business practices. I flipped to another picture of him holding up a championship trophy in full hockey gear with the rest of his charity ice hockey team. There was a real man, I thought, giving some side-eye to Blandy across the table.

I could not have a crush on my boss. He was a titan of industry, a billionaire CEO who had built his conglomerate corporation from nothing. He had a wicked sense of humor and a hand that had been firm on mine. I apologized for checking my email and gave Blandy my attention.

This had to stop. I could not keep thinking of the head of the company that employed me in a sexual way. I wondered what he could do with that luscious mouth of his and then blinked too fast in hopes that Blandy didn't think I looked turned on by him. I told him that I was going to have to make it an early night. I even insisted on paying for my half of dinner and told him I'd call soon if I had a chance. I shook his hand. He stayed to finish his dinner. I felt confident that he was as underwhelmed by me as I was with him.

In the Uber home, I texted my friends that I had a super boring date and had to stop crushing on my boss before I was caught drawing his initials in a heart on my notebook. I resolved to stop thinking of him that way. I had a job to do, and there was hardly a reason for me to run into him, speak with him, or even think of him again.

But twenty minutes later, I was between the sheets and sure as hell wasn't thinking of Blandy when I reached in the nightstand for my favorite vibrator. I knew what I needed, why I felt so restless. I'd basically had a lady hard-on since my conversation with Brent in his office that morning. So it was time to get this devil off my shoulder and get myself off. I could put the whole sordid fantasy of my boss in the past and turn over a new leaf. A professional leaf. A leaf that didn't ogle executives at my place of work.

I stripped off my tank top and ran my hands over my bare breasts, stroking and teasing them until my nipples were rock hard. I plucked at them, rubbed them with my thumbs, felt myself breathing harder, the rise and fall of my flushed chest moving faster. I felt chills ripple over my body as my hand slid down my belly and into my panties. The purple lace ones I'd wasted on a date with Blandy. I banished the thought of him instantly since he was the opposite of sexy to me.

Instead, I let my eyes drift shut on the image of Brent Waltham hoisting a championship trophy in hockey gear, followed by Brent reaching for my hand, Brent calling me out about being on my phone in a meeting. Oh, that was the one---to the wicked fantasy that he might have told me to see him in his office after the meeting, like a stern professor who intended to punish me. Punish me by driving me wild and making me wait and wait before he'd let me come. A shiver went through me at the first touch of my fingers to my clit as I spread myself and pressed the humming vibrator right where I liked it. I gritted my teeth, unnerved by how fast I was fully aroused. I was usually a slow burn girl, but I was going full throttle after how keyed up I'd been all day.

It was the thought of our banter, our witty conversation escalating to something more heated. The spark of lust was there, and the stimulating way he talked with me fired up my entire body. As we teased each other, as I met him sarcastic remark for sarcastic remark, we'd step closer to one another. The rippling heat between us drawing us like magnets. Our breath would come harder. I would hold up one hand, press it to his chest and find it firm and muscular as it looked. He would take me by the hips, his hands drawing me against him so our bodies met at full length.

Breathless with desire, with the taste of him hot and sweet as his tongue parted my lips wider so he could slide his tongue in my mouth. I would moan, tilt my head and take the stroke of his tongue gladly, touching the tip of my tongue to his lip, tentative before the urgent mating of our mouths took over. His hands would open my blouse, palms covering my breasts as my nipples pebbled in response. I would reach up for his shoulders and hold on to them like they were my anchor. The heavy, muscular shoulders under my hands would feel like paradise, and he would lift me onto that desk of his and push my skirt up. His fingers would find my lace panties and push them aside, stroking and petting me as I writhed, helpless, and clutched at his shoulders and his neck.

He would pull away from me to put his face between my legs and lick me once in a long, hot stroke with the flat of his tongue that made my core seize and clench. Then he would stand and open his pants, his long cock hard for me. Before I could say a word, he would see me reaching for him, my arms outstretched. He would give me what I wanted, his big cock easing into me inch by thick, mouth-watering inch until he filled me to the hilt and I bowed up off the desk, gasping as I tried to take all of him. My fists would clench uselessly and pound the desktop as he thrust his hips forward and I took the heavy pressure of his cock driving into me. His thumb would flick across my clit like a kiss. I would come hard and tight around him, crying out and surging up into his arms. Brent would hold me and pump into me, his own climax following fast, his powerful body shuddering against me. I would wrap my legs around him, pinning him against me as close as we could be. My legs would be weak and shaky as I tried to slide off the desk.

He would help me straighten my clothing as my pussy clenched with shivering aftershocks from the deep, satisfying orgasm he'd given me. I would have dick withdrawal immediately and want more of it like a junkie. I would be pulling at his shirt, urging him to unbutton it so I could rub my hands on his chest with nothing between us. Then he'd dip his head and kiss me softly and slowly and tell me what a lovely meeting it had been.

I came all over the vibrator and my own probing fingers. I felt wrung out by my orgasm, a little frustrated that it had happened so quickly, but I had lingered there, finished the fantasy I was telling myself in the afterglow. I wanted to go again, that's how wound up I was over him, but I stopped at one. I had work in the morning and needed my sleep. Even if it was destined to be restless and full of vivid sex dreams about my boss.

This was supposed to get the foolish crush out of my system by entertaining a single detailed fantasy, going to town with my vibrator and considering the entire episode nothing more than an embarrassing infatuation on my first job. Instead, it had sharpened my hunger for him. It had made me realize this was more than a crush. I took out the issue of Forbes I kept in my bedside table—hey, some women have PornHub, I have Forbes—and gazed at the cover. I felt a warm fondness for the man in the photo as well as the familiar, visceral physical reaction to it. I didn't actually kiss his picture good night because *that* would've been ridiculous.

I lay there, spent, and just longed for him. I let myself drift off to sleep, wondering what it would be like to have him there with me. I woke up feeling comforted and happy.

Then memory came sliding back in. I squinted my eyes shut in dismay. I should never have indulged in graphic fantasies about my boss. Now I wouldn't be able to look at him without blushing.

Building my career was the focus right now, not masturbating to thoughts of Brent. Damn. Just the memory of his laugh gave me tingles in places I could not allow to tingle. Something about it being forbidden just made it worse. Or better. Because my body was humming, my nipples coming to sharp peaks that begged to be pinched, a heavy dampness between my legs.

In for a penny, in for a pound, I reasoned and reached for my vibrator. I was shameless. I was going to rub one out before work, just thinking of him.

6

BRENT

After my morning run, I messaged Millie to have all of HR full-time staff waiting in the conference room by nine. We had a situation to address. I might have to switch to yoga because I could definitely see myself developing high blood pressure if shit like this kept coming up.

I was a businessman, an award winner, renowned for my environmentally-conscious practices. I was not going to destroy that reputation by beating the hell out of an executive VP who deserved it richly. Despite the fact it would have given me great satisfaction. Those marketing sons of bitches always had been trouble. They had that used car salesman shine, but with higher salaries and apparently a bad case of entitlement.

My reflection showed a perfectly tailored gray suit, Italian leather wingtips gleaming as I straightened my dark purple tie. I took a long drink of water because there might be shouting, and I didn't want my throat to grow dry. I wasn't a bellower as a general rule. I led with dispassionate practicality. Most of the time. This kind of crap made me furious though.

The conference table was lined with solemn-faced human resources employees. I turned to Herb Rosings, my executive VP of HR.

"I expect you've told them what this is about?" I said. He nodded.

"The unfortunate situation with Maxwell, sir."

"Yes. Although I'm inclined to refer to it as the felony recently committed—allegedly committed by our soon-to-be-former executive VP of marketing. In looking over his HR file, I found three previous complaints against him by female employees junior to him. In one case, it was a direct report below him, so she was reassigned to a different supervisor, but she resigned the next year. The other two involved women in the same department, an intern and an assistant. He was reprimanded and sent for sensitivity training and sexual harassment training, correct?" I said, already knowing the answer.

"Yes," Herb said.

"So now he's sexually assaulted an intern *in this building*." My voice rose of its own volition. "One of the interns in my company has been abused by an executive within the offices of this corporation, here on site. Under our noses, you might say. My information here is incomplete. She did not report this to law enforcement?"

"No, sir. The young woman, er—"

"The victim, Herb. She is the victim of a sexual assault carried out by Josh Maxwell from Marketing in the goddamn men's room on the thirty-seventh floor. Her name?"

"Mariah Ross," Herb said faintly, "I met her a few times. Soft-spoken, seemed like a hard worker."

I groaned loudly, showing my frustration. "Forgive me, I

find that my professional objectivity is clouded on this issue. I'm angry," I said.

"No apology necessary," Kim said. "We're all mad as hell. What I want to know is what we're doing about Maxwell?"

"Apart from firing him? Destroying his professional reputation and making him unemployable in North America and Europe? I'll speak with legal later on, but I plan to sue him for both breach of contract and gross misconduct."

"Shouldn't PR be up here? To discuss how to spin this story?"

"There is no spin. An employee of Astley Corp has been terminated due to sexual harassment and a lawsuit is pending. There's the story."

"Brent," Kim said patiently, "what are we doing to make sure that Mariah is taken care of and so she doesn't sue Astley?"

"Astley is going to back her. We will go on record as being on her side, and provide a crack legal team to represent her as co-plaintiff against Maxwell. She gets all of the financial settlement. We'll just light the torches and lead the mob," I said decisively.

"That is—perhaps you should discuss this strategy with legal," Kim said carefully.

"I intend to do so. But first, we need to review the current state of our sexual harassment training and reporting procedures. This can't be allowed to happen again. I want to know what the options are with respect to reworking our policy to discipline and potentially punish offenders," I said.

"What about educating them?" Cat interrupted. "I mean, I get wanting to punish them, because what they did was wrong and an abuse of power. If they are trained properly to recognize what is acceptable versus what is intimidating or harmful, and assessed on it, they can be required to attain a certain score. This would also qualify in due process as being made aware of conduct expectations explicitly and with a paper trail. So if there's an infraction, cut it down to one warning with remediation followed by resignation with a poor reference."

"I like that idea. We'd need to engage a consultant on sexual harassment training, bring in experts, have a multi-day seminar with clear examples and scenarios. Make a note of that, Herb."

Herb obediently wrote it down while Millie scrawled it on the whiteboard she'd wheeled in for brainstorming purposes. We tossed around a variety of ideas on how to deal with violations of our policy going forward and possible rewording of the policy to make it more specific and actionable. An appendix needed to be added to all hiring contracts in this regard. All current employees and contractors needed updated training and verification.

I had Millie book a meeting in the afternoon with legal and another with finance to allocate a budget to the training program. It was all a massive headache. Anyone with common decency would have known better than to corner and intern and feel her up, for God's sake. Ruining his name, reputation, and financial situation seemed inadequate, but it would have to do.

After adjourning the meeting, I asked Kim and Cat to come to my office to discuss their ideas further. Kim's conservative bent would temper my rashness in the situation. She always gave sound counsel, and Cat had had good ideas in the meeting. I poured them each a glass of water and thanked them for their input.

"As a recent graduate, Ms. Sherman, you're up to date on the industry-standard definitions of sexual harassment as well as initiatives to eliminate it. I read the professional publications, of course, and watch the news, but I'd be interested to hear a fresh perspective," I said.

"Well, what I understand is that women of my generation are benefiting from the burgeoning attitude that this mistreatment isn't something we have to endure and pretend to ignore. It's all the time, wherever we go, the grocery store, a club, the train—men staring, chatting us up, asking personal questions, making remarks about our appearance. All of this unsolicited sexual attention. The old school view of sexual harassment was just a boss chasing his secretary around the desk—not being crowded against a wall while he shoves his hand up your skirt. But it happens a great deal. The definition is evolving, and I do think an ongoing conversation about acceptable versus unacceptable behavior at work needs to happen. Like, save your dirty jokes for when you're off the clock. Never remark on the body of a coworker. Never refer to their private life or sexuality or gender identification. It's stuff like that, things the generation in positions of power doesn't really equate with harassment."

I watched her, the way she gestured with her hands, the authority of her speaking voice, how articulate she was. She was impressive. I nodded my head in agreement. Kim chimed in.

"We need to clarify and expand the definition, as Cat suggests, and try to keep complaints of this nature private, both to protect the victim and to keep the public image of the company from being corroded. You can't expect to recruit excellent staff if you're known as the sexual harassment company or the corporation that can't seem to solve this workplace problem. You don't want stockholders or potential employees to associate your brand with the words sexual harassment at all that's one reason I am against a lawsuit. You think you'll be a white knight and swing the sword of justice or something, but all you're going to do is dirty your hands with this, Brent," she said.

"I see your point, and I'll discuss it with legal before doing anything rash, but I'm confident that stockholders and the board of directors as well would weigh in on this in favor of punishing wrongdoing and taking a stand."

"Excuse me, I have to take this call," Kim said, stepping out of the office.

"I can't believe you let her use her phone in a meeting," Cat said mischievously.

"She's a senior department head. There are perks to that level of achievement," I replied easily.

"No reprimand? No demand to know what she's talking about?" she said cheekily, "or do you reserve public embarrassment for the new hires?"

"No, it's a gift I extend to all my staff. If you can't stand up for yourself, you don't belong at Astley Corp. It's no place for the weak-willed."

"So it's a weeding out process? If I had burst into tears, would I have lost my job?"

"Not immediately, but you would have been under suspicion of being too delicate to survive in the corporate world."

"Did I pass the test?" she countered.

"You're still here, aren't you? In a meeting in the executive suite, being asked to consult on a heavy matter of employee misconduct."

"Yes, I am."

"I think we should continue the discussion over lunch.

Would you care to join me?" I said. I admitted to myself that I wanted very much for her to say yes.

"Why, Mr. Waltham, are you harassing me in the workplace? Suggesting that my privileged spot at the table on this important topic is contingent upon my willingness to have a private 'lunch' with you?" she asked.

"Absolutely not," I said, stepping back behind my desk so it was between us, "It would seem I need retraining myself. I had no intention of coercing or intimidating you into—"

"Oh my god, you should see your face! I was joking!" she laughed.

Her entire face lit with amusement. Her laugh wasn't musical or dainty—it was loud and full-throated and husky. I was arrested by the sound of it, the vision of her so joyful and mischievous.

"Well played," I acknowledged.

She dropped a curtsey and rolled her eyes, "I accept the lunch invitation. I'm starving."

I was surprised she agreed to go. I was downright astonished she had joked about harassment seconds after a deadly serious conversation about the same subject. I was thunderstruck that I had met someone as irreverent as I was.

"You know, joking about serious subjects can get you into trouble at work," I told her.

"I'm pretty good at reading a room," she remarked rather too wisely for my taste. She was so young, so inexperienced to see through me so well.

"That you are," I admitted, "after you, Miss Sherman."

She led the way to the elevator. As the doors slid shut, she gave me a sidelong glance, "Easily one of the top three elevators," she said.

Part of me knew she was joking. Some other part of me

stepped out of the shadows and wanted to say something about knowing how to make it her number one elevator in history, but I would be damned if I'd overstep boundaries with an employee. So I kept uncomfortably to my side of the elevator and willed it to descend faster so I could be free of this confined space where I could have easily reached out to touch her, to lay claim to her.

Damn my thoughts and urges. Damn Kim for having a personal call. Damn me for suggesting lunch. It was going to be an awkward hour that much was certain.

7

———

CAT

He opened my car door.

Probably the last man who opened a car door for me was my daddy. He did that the day I graduated high school—drove me right up to the gym door, stopped, got out of the driver's side and came around and opened my door like I was a lady, not a seventeen year old in confetti pink lip gloss wearing flip flops with her cap and gown.

So when Brent Waltham, who had a literal driver of his own, paused and opened my door before going around to get in the car himself, it caught me off guard. I wasn't expecting him to be chivalrous. He had won me over pretty instantly by treating me as an equal so acting gentlemanly, treating me with a type of consideration that underlined my femininity made me feel---girly. Flattered and like if I had a lace fan in an old fashioned movie, I'd be fluttering that bitch for all I was worth.

Riding with him was basically torture. We sat as far apart as the back seat would allow. I fastened my safety belt and sat with my ankles crossed, hands primly in my lap. I remarked on the weather and how nice it was not to have to

44

call an Uber. He said that it was supposed to rain sometime after six. We lapsed into silence. He was making and unmaking fists. When my eyes drifted to his hands, I saw that they were white at the knuckles. His smooth bronze skin gone pale because he clenched his fingers so tightly.

"You okay?" I inquired.

"Hmm?" he said as though deep in thought.

"Your knuckles are white," I pointed out helpfully.

"Oh," he said, a little abashed, and unclenched his fists with effort. "I suppose the Maxwell incident has me on edge. It's a difficult topic because it makes me angry personally. I pride myself on maintaining a pragmatic and professional stance. Not to involve emotion."

"Okay, I watched Tough Guise in my gender communications class. I know pretending to have no emotions or compartmentalizing them is a common thing, but I don't understand it. How do you not feel things? When Kim told me just the basics of what happened with Maxwell, it made my skin crawl. I wanted to throw up. I wanted to punch the guy in the face repeatedly. I was sick and angry and just disgusted so if you felt that way or any other way about it, it's human. Why are we asking men not to be human and feel things?"

"It isn't a *lack* of emotions, it's a restriction of them. Feelings are something private and aren't expressed in public that's how I have always experienced it."

"That makes more sense, but I still couldn't live like that. It's such a harmful stereotype. I mean, guys can show anger or indignation in public, but that's about it. What happened to joy or grief or passion?"

"Those are private."

"That's just—archaic," I said with a light laugh as we took out our menus.

We had a table by a window in a very nice restaurant. It was beautiful and elegant, but not uncomfortably fancy. There were green plants in the corners, a small cactus on each table, everything else cream-colored and crisp.

"I like it here. Very pretty," I said, noticing ferns and orchid, a feeling of lightness and nature.

He nodded without looking up from his menu. I liked that, because this was business. I looked over the menu and settled on the herbed salmon with jasmine rice. After we ordered, he looked at me almost purposefully.

"I'd like you to elaborate on what you said in the meeting about more specific training. I think it would be useful for me to know some scenarios—I have been meticulous in my career to avoid any kind of ambiguous or sexual interactions with employees, but there is as you said more to it than the obvious."

He seemed to falter, to be unsure. It stunned me that the most confident, impressive man I'd ever known was uncertain about something.

"Well, okay, the bywords here are reasonable and consent. If a reasonable person would take action, then you're probably okay. Like when we were in the car if the driver slammed on the breaks to avoid an accident, and I grabbed your arm. That would be a reaction that a reasonable person might make and immediately let go. But if he slammed on the breaks—"

"And if I used the opportunity to touch your breast, that would be unreasonable. I might throw out my arm to stop you from lurching forward, but coping an opportunistic feel would be over the line. I think that's obvious."

"Yes. And if we were attending a funeral for a board member or something, a solemn post-work occasion, and you put your arm around the widow to comfort her when she cried, that's normal. If you grabbed her ass—inappropriate," I snickered, "or if you seemed upset during the funeral, which you obviously wouldn't because you're devoid of feelings—and I covered your hand with mine like this," I reached across the table and laid my hand on his, squeezed his fingers a little.

My sentence trailed off. My eyes tracked to the spot where I held his hand. There was energy there. That was the best word I could come up with for it. Energy crackling off that touch, that perfectly commonplace, platonic touch.

His thumb skated across my palm and I rolled my lips under and bit them in response. He was holding my hand, stroking my palm with one thumb. If we had been at a funeral, the entire interaction would have communicated —'it's okay, have a tissue' and 'thanks, that's kind of you.' But in a restaurant, across a table from my billionaire boss whose most basic gaze set my skin on fire, the touches said something more like, 'oh god that feels good' and 'if you think that feels good, how about I stroke you like this?' I swear to God, I wanted to moan. Hence biting my own lips to keep from it.

Obviously, I should have withdrawn my hand, the point made or not about casual, not sexually charged contact, but I wouldn't deny myself. I let myself have this one moment. This breathless moment where I had laid my hand atop his and squeezed his fingers only to have him rake his thumb back and forth across my innocent, unsuspecting, hopelessly horny fingers. If I groaned, 'oh god yes,' that would be embarrassing. I swallowed the words with great effort. Every single part of my body down to the soles of my feet prickled with an awareness of him. My pulse was throbbing in my throat. I knew if he looked up at my neck he would see the pounding of my heart visible there beneath my pale skin.

"And would this be reasonable? If I caught your hand and held it?" he asked archly. I cleared my throat.

"That brings us to the second key word. Consent. It's likely very rare for there to be a mutual attraction between coworkers of unequal positions of power, but ending harassment doesn't end romance. It makes it better because we're sexual beings," my eyes skidded to his face. Not one eyelash betrayed a reaction to my use of the words.

"And we can speak about our desires. If the other person wants it, too, then they say so. You have to have enthusiastic consent. Consent isn't 'I guess' consent is 'yes, more, please.'" I said. I breathed the last few words, my voice husky.

"So if I held your hand, the simple act of not taking back your hand isn't consent? The fact that you gripped my fingers tighter, as if you'd never let go? The way you bit your lips and then licked them? Are those not nonverbal cues to continue?"

"They could be, or they could be reluctant or have a fear of retribution. It could be arousal or it could be fear. Silence, freezing, not speaking up, those can be responses to a threat as well."

"But I'm no threat to you. You have as much power as I have in the interaction. 'Yes' was waiting on your tongue. I could feel it, and I could hear it," he said. His voice, oh God, his voice! I could feel his voice sliding up and down my chest. I wanted to lick the sound of it, dark and glorious, but I had a point to make, and I was nothing if not stubborn.

"You could easily be a threat to me. You could force me. You could retaliate if I refused. You could hurt me physically or ruin me professionally. Barter prestigious assignments and promotions or threaten termination or loss of privileges—there's so much power you could leverage over me in your position so much that would make a woman afraid to say no, or feeling like she couldn't afford to. That's coercion."

"A real man doesn't need to coerce a woman. He offers. And she accepts."

"What if she doesn't accept?" I challenged.

"I've never experienced that," he said plainly. And I felt it straight down to my bones.

"I bet you haven't," I sighed.

"Why do you say that?"

"Oh, it isn't acceptable to make remarks about a coworker's physical appearance. So no comment," I said.

"I asked. You're allowed to answer. I won't report you," he teased.

"You're—" I chose my words carefully— 'your appearance might be defined as classically handsome." It sounded wooden, hollow in my ears, too cold a description.

"I see. So I might be categorized as having symmetrical features?"

"Exactly," I laughed.

"Say what you want to say, Cat. You don't have to hold your breath around me," he said. God, that was appealing. A man who wasn't going to take offense if I misspoke or if I joked about something serious. I smiled in spite of myself.

"Okay, you look like pretty much every red-blooded woman's fantasy. Like George Clooney would play second fiddle to you," I finished, surprised as hell that I was that open and honest. Even though he'd asked for it. What the hell was I doing?

"Clooney's a distant second? I'll tell him that in person at the next fundraiser," he chuckled.

My face must've turned as red as it did hot because Brent broke into shoulder shaking laughter. "Don't worry, I won't actually say tell him that."

"Oh good," I said. "I wouldn't want to have to change my name and move to a new country to escape the embarrassment."

Brent chuckled. "You'd be surprised how low key and self-deprecating George is about his looks."

With a half-smile, he released my hand as our food arrived. My hand felt cold without the grip of his, but the rest of my body was warm with the knowledge that I wanted him. I knew it couldn't go anywhere, but the fact that he knew how attractive I found him infused every minute with possibility. We ate our food and spoke of other scenarios calmly.

"In an elevator," he said, the spark in his eyes mischievous, "if you're alone with a member of the opposite sex, and by mutual admission, there is an attraction, what is the appropriate course to take? You have perhaps ninety seconds before the doors open."

"A lot can happen in ninety seconds," I managed, taking a sip of my chardonnay.

"Such as? Fingers trailing down your neck, my hand sliding beneath your hair, tipping your face upward?"

"That would be inappropriate," I answered, barely able to speak. I felt sparks along my skin where he had suggested touching me. My scalp seemed to tighten, my chest rising, even heaving with a heavy breath.

"Would it still be inappropriate if I said 'may I?' first and you said yes?"

"No. Consent is the deciding factor."

"Or is desire the deciding factor?" he challenged. Something rose in me then.

"Desire is subjective. You might think someone wanted you because you were projecting that or because of your ego rather than reality."

"What about a purely biological response?" he teased, the curve to his lips absolutely filthy with suggestion.

"You'd be hard-pressed to find a woman with eyes who didn't react to you biologically."

"Are you speaking from experience?"

I nearly spit my wine out at the question. What the hell was going on? Was he really flirting this hard with me? And why? Surely there were women all over town willing to throw themselves at Brent. Why would he be pressing little old me so hard? Unless it was a joke of some sort. I almost looked around to see if there was someone with a camera hiding behind the fern in the corner.

"Your cheeks are flushed," he pointed out ruthlessly.

"No kidding," I said.

"Am I making you uncomfortable?" he asked honestly.

"No. You just caught me off guard for a moment," I said, trying to regain my composure.

"You're not clutching your pearls," he said teasingly.

"Just let me pretend I am, okay? I'm new to this job and not looking for a way to screw it up. I like my life and my career path. I don't have any intentions of doing anything to jeopardize what I've worked pretty damn hard for."

"Honorable," he said lightly.

"Are you making fun of me?" I asked, feigning offense.

"Not at all. I find it oddly refreshing that you aren't willing to trade sex for opportunity at work."

"No. I think that's demeaning to my education and the hard work I've put into establishing a good working reputation for myself."

"I agree, it would be, but what if I were to tell you that if anything consensual were to happen, it wouldn't affect your status at the workplace?"

I regarded him for a moment before answering. "So we sleep together and nothing at work changes?"

"If that were an option?"

I shook my head. "I don't think it's possible, or at least not for me."

"Noted."

We went back to our meal silently for a few minutes, but I barely tasted my food as my mind raced over our conversation. What the actual fuck was happening here? We'd gone from a meeting on sexual harassment in the workplace to lunch to discuss implementing policy and ended up talking about sex.

As if sensing my thoughts spinning out of control, Brent cleared his throat to get my attention.

"Cat. Is it short for Catherine?" he asked.

"No. Caitlin."

"Caitlin. That's lovely. It also sounds incredibly young if I'm honest."

"I'm twenty-four."

"Jesus, when you say that, I feel ancient.

I laughed. "Forty-seven isn't ancient," I said.

He leveled me with a look of surprise. "How did you know how old I am?"

I blushed again and before I could answer that I was basically a psycho stalker with his picture taped to my ceiling, he waved a hand.

"Never mind. So tell me about growing up in your small town. Tell me about you."

"I have five brothers, so I'm an expert referee. I'm good at making deals, enforcing them. I was a natural for HR. For judging character and negotiating differences."

"The only girl in a houseful of boys? I guess you learned to hold your own."

"Yeah, pretty quickly. And I'm the youngest so my parents had already gotten used to raising boys. I wasn't going to wear hair bows and be afraid of getting dirty that was for sure. They raised me to believe I could do anything the boys could."

"Sounds like it was a good childhood."

"It was. What about you?"

"I was raised by my grandmother. We didn't have much, but she instilled a strong work ethic in me. I started working when I was fifteen and I've never stopped."

"That's directly from an interview you did," I said, "what's the real story?"

He chuckled. "I grew up wanting to prove I didn't need my parents or anyone else. And I have. I didn't start with nothing, because I had a grandmother who loved me and made sure I did my homework and ate supper every night. And that was what kept me from screwing up my life too much—not wanting to disappoint her after everything she sacrificed to keep me. She was my dad's mother. He was back in jail by the time I was born, and my mother was some girl he sold drugs to, who left me on his doorstep when I was a baby."

"I'm sorry," I said. "I had no idea. I guess the magazines make it sound like they were noble people who died in an accident or something."

"It's not something I publicize, although he was a pretty successful dealer before he got busted, so maybe my business sense was inherited," he said ruefully.

"My mom is a peacemaker, so that's probably where I get my people skills, but my stubbornness was entirely learned from dealing with my brothers. Especially Ben. He has to have the last word no matter what. I mean, there were days that if I was big enough, I would've thrown him right through a window," I laughed.

"So that's one of your negotiating tactics? Throwing out the window?"

"No, I'd need a burly assistant to do the actual throwing. It's a goal of mine career-wise, to hire a former bouncer to be my secretary. Then they can toss people outside for me when I'm fed up," I said. He laughed.

"So putting your office on an upper floor may have been a mistake."

"That depends on how you look at it. If your chronic complainers to HR who don't like how their coworker's coffee smells or don't like the music that someone listens to —if those people get tossed out an upper window, I'm not even sorry."

"Note to self, send new hires for empathy training," he quipped.

"Right," I said, "So, you're divorced."

"Wow. That was one hell of a transition," he said.

"Okay, I can be direct. I want to know. Since the whole raised by the grandmother after an accident bit was fake, what about the divorce? Was it real?"

"Unfortunately, yes. It was years ago. The main problem there was that our expectations didn't match. I was working eighteen-hour days plus, and she didn't like being left alone in a penthouse and maybe seeing me a couple of days a week for an hour or two here and there. We'd have Sunday brunch, but she spent it complaining that I was never around, and I spent it ignoring her and figuring out how long I had to sit there before I could leave."

"Sounds romantic. Why did you get married then?"

"She was pregnant," he said matter of factly.

"Oh. I wasn't aware you had a child."

"I don't."

"I'm sorry," I said, feeling bad for prying.

"Thank you. We had been together for a few months, and she was pregnant so we went to the courthouse. There was a miscarriage, but we decided to stay together. On my part, I didn't want to be a quitter. I didn't want her to feel like losing the baby was some kind of failure of hers or that she'd lose me over it. Although she never had me, not really so I married her for bad reasons. Then she found other men to pay attention to her when I was gone too much. It isn't even an original story."

"I'm sorry," I said again, "about your child."

"Thanks. I haven't told that story very often. My friend Malcolm knows. And now you know. An employee I just met," he shook his head ruefully.

"Hopefully I'm more than just an employee," I said robustly.

"Friends?"

"Yes. Brent," I said, speaking his name to make him smile a little. "See, first name basis. Plus we held hands and we talked about our personal lives. So that's friendship."

"It is?"

"Why? What do you think it is?"

"Answer something for me, before I agree to being friends."

"All right."

"If you didn't work for me, would you consider going home with me?"

Again, I was caught off guard. "I'm not sure. I don't have a blueprint for this. I haven't found myself in this situation often enough to deal with it gracefully. The work thing is part of it, but another part of it is shame, feeling like I haven't known you long enough, we're not seriously dating one another, so I'm not supposed to go back to go home with you, so to speak."

"Supposed to? How disappointing. Just when I had you pegged for a divergent thinker, you've fallen for the oppressive system of shame and judging a woman's value by her purported innocence. Here's the truth, adult men don't want to sleep with virgins. We want women who know what they like. Women who say what they mean, and know their way around our bodies as well."

"If you have a dating seminar, sign me up," I said.

"I might give private lessons," he said, his voice low.

"You can just turn anything into a proposition, can't you?" I laughed. "Is that how you got ahead in business?"

"Yes. A very large number of sexual favors. The secret to my success," he deadpanned.

I grinned. Talking with him was exhilarating and intimate. I felt fizzy inside from all the flirting and teasing, and I felt confident, powerful. Like I was singled out as interesting and worth his time. I gave him a smile and sipped my wine. There was a lot left in the glass, so the buzz in my head had nothing to do with alcohol. It was all Brent Waltham.

"I have your Forbes cover. At my apartment. It has moved with me since I lived in a dorm."

"You're kidding."

"No."

"Why did you save it?"

I stared at him. I should not have started this line of conversation.

"I read it for the articles," I said archly.

"Oh, really? So I *am* your George Clooney?"

"If I admitted such a ridiculous thing, it would give you far too much power," I said evasively.

"Just about enough power, I'd say. That would be if it were hypothetically true, the single most flattering thing anyone has ever said to me. That a gorgeous young girl has kept my magazine cover because she likes to—"

"Read the articles, like I said," I gave him a sly smile.

"So how often do you read those articles?" he teased.

"Well, let's see, I read them last night until I was worn out. And when I woke up this morning, I couldn't resist reading them again really quickly."

"Really? Twice in twelve hours. You must enjoy that issue."

"No one has ever enjoyed a back issue of Forbes more than me," I said with a smile.

8

BRENT

I met with legal, took their more conservative advice reluctantly. Kim had been right of course—a rash action would reflect poorly on the company. Maxwell would be well and truly punished and the victim would be supported and taken care of.

All through that meeting, I had difficulty focusing, which was unusual for me, but my thoughts kept drifting back to my long lunch with Cat. Not just her ideas, but the way it felt when she gripped my fingers, the honest way she shared her thoughts. The way her mind worked and how she had been so responsive to my every suggestion. Riding the elevator to my office had elicited a sharp intake of breath on my part. I could imagine it so clearly, lying naked with Cat in the bedroom. She would be lying on my bare chest, and I would be toying with her nipple—those nipples that had poked so sharply through her silky blouse at lunch, hardening whenever I mentioned anything suggestive. How they would feel in my mouth, how enticing it would be to have her come to me and say she had changed her mind. She would slowly open one button after another, starting at her throat. I would suck her neck there where she revealed bare skin, and then her collarbone, the valley between her breasts, the curve of her stomach. I was sweating. One of the lawyers was talking, and I broke out in a sweat from the fantasy I was letting unfold during a meeting.

I got a glass of water and drained it to cool myself down. In the span of that lunch we shared, she had risen in my estimation from an articulate young hire in HR to a woman I'd told secrets to. A woman I was so attracted to that I had begun to trust her because my lust for her was so powerful it clouded my thinking. She knew that I had only gotten married because of a pregnancy and that a part of me still mourned that lost child. And that I was willing to joke around and flirt during a serious discussion of evolving sexual harassment policies. I took a lot of risks with her. I told her things she could take to a tabloid and have a million dollars in her account before midnight. I propositioned her openly and admitted to it. She could sue me and the company for soliciting sexual favors from her.

I had given her far more power to ruin my reputation than I could have imagined. Scorching lust made me careless. Somehow it had been so long since I'd wanted anyone so much, that the experience, just the core physical reaction I had to her made me reckless. I had said all manner of inappropriate things to her. I had stroked her knuckles in a way that I wanted to stroke between her legs, imagining how my thumb could drag slowly across every plump, wet fold, parting her. It was excruciating.

After I finished with legal and PR came in with the statement they'd developed for a press release, I left to go home. I had Millie cancel the dinner I was scheduled to attend. I needed time to myself, to think. I had stupidly risked my career, the career I'd spent decades building, by saying indiscreet things to a new hire. I wanted to call her in a panic and demand that she does not tell a soul, but if she hadn't thought of the money she stood to make off of the conversation at lunch, I didn't want to tip her off by giving her the idea. Not that Cat wasn't clever enough to come up with a hustle on her own. I just hoped that she was sincerely interested in me that her biological reaction could be developed into more than that, into a full-fledged love affair. I hadn't had a lover in two months since I broke it off with Riley, who thought we should take our relationship public.

To have Cat for my lover, I would have given up a great deal. I acknowledged that to myself. She made me feel alive, awake, made me *want* again. It didn't bear thinking about that what I wanted from Cat wasn't just sex. I craved connection. I craved her words, her facial expressions, her laughter. I craved all of her.

9

CAT

My friend Sarah Jo thought it was insane that I had flirted with my boss over a sexual harassment policy lunch meeting, but she already knew I was crazy to start with. She told me to go for it. Of course, she was always good at wanting other people to be happy, taking care of her friends and family before herself. So if I was having earth-shaking orgasms with my famous boss, maybe she'd feel like that was one more person she could check off of her list whose happiness she thought she was responsible for.

Work in HR was at a fever pitch. We were constantly researching, interviewing consultants and working on copy for our revamped policies. Lunch had become salads eaten out of plastic containers with one hand while on the phone or tablet. I went out with Heather and some other friends a few times, once to a paint and wine party that involved a lot more wine than decent artwork. Predictably, Blandy had never called me back, which was fine by me. One of the guys who frequented the coffee place near my apartment had asked me out. I had managed a halfhearted refusal about how I was busy with work. The truth was, I loved my job. My coworkers were smart and interesting, and I liked hanging out with them. And all the sexual tension and excitement I needed was available in the executive suite.

I had only sat in on one other meeting with Brent. He spent a lot of time closeted with legal and the COO. Kim referred to it as crisis mode. When she went to his office, she was summoned alone. New hires didn't get to tag along so at the end of the day on a Thursday, I grabbed a flyer for a new client discount at a chiropractor and rode up in the elevator.

Brent and I had barely spoken in over a week. A hello in the hallway, a nod. Part of me was smug that I had managed not to sleep with him the day we went to lunch since clearly, it was a whim and not a lasting interest in who I was. The rest of me knew he was busy and stubbornly believed there was a connection between us, however unlikely and fast that might seem to the rational part of my brain.

Millie was away from her desk, so I buzzed his office myself and said it was important; that I had something to deliver in person. He told me to press the button on the underside of Millie's desk and come in. He was alone.

Brent stood when I entered. He was wearing a suit, of course, and his hair was slightly disheveled—that face, so familiar from pictures, so much more gorgeous and mobile in person, made me stop and stare. He was even taller than I remembered, bigger somehow. He was imposing even though he had loomed large in my memory all that time.

"Good afternoon, Cat. What important message are you here to deliver?"

"This," I said, holding out the flier. He chuckled and tossed it on his desk, which was far more cluttered with papers and electronic devices than when I'd visited previously.

"You look tired," I said, taking a step closer. He shoved his hands in his pockets and shrugged.

"It's been a long... week? Has it been longer than that?" he said, sounding exhausted.

I went to him then and looked up into his face, the lines around his eyes, the hint of disappointment or sadness there. I didn't reach for him and hold him, though I wanted to. He wasn't mine to hold. He wasn't mine at all so I touched his face. He flinched at first, then his eyes dropped shut. He let me lay my hand on his cheek. My fingers stroked the hair at his temple, and he sighed.

Brent took his hands from his pockets. His hand closed around my wrist, held my hand to his face for an instant before pushing me away.

"Not a good idea," he said, "but thank you."

Something, some feeling welled in me then. I wondered how long it had been since anyone had touched him with affection, with consideration, or at all. I longed to put my arms around him. But he had put me away, and I had to walk the walk on consent as well. No matter what I wanted or how strongly I wanted him.

"You're not even going to read the top-secret information I brought you?" I teased, trying to lighten the mood.

"If you think you need an excuse to come to my office and see me, you're wrong."

"If you believe that, *you're* wrong that secretary has turned me away this week already, said you were busy."

"I was busy. But I would have seen you anyway."

"Why?" I said before I could stop myself.

"Because we're friends, remember?" he said lightly.

"I seem to remember something about that, but I don't know if Millie gives a crap if I think we're friends."

He buzzed his secretary and asked her to come in. Millie rushed in, tablet in hand, ready for instructions.

"Millie, this is Cat Sherman from HR. She's working on a special project for me so she'll need to be admitted to my office regardless of my schedule until further notice."

"Yes, sir," Millie said. "Is that all?"

"Yes, thank you. Feel free to go home early. Put the phones on voicemail. It's been a long week."

"Yes, it has. You should get some rest," she said, concern on her face. He gave a shrug, and she closed the door as she left.

"Special project?" I giggled.

"Yes, you're finding me the best chiropractor in the city. This pamphlet is only the first of your research artifacts. You have to keep me updated daily on your progress."

"Daily? As in you want to see me every day?" I said, almost in disbelief.

"I've wanted to see you every day," he said.

"Yeah, I'm sure you sat in meetings with the COO and all those other initials and thought, oh I wish that new girl from HR was here," I laughed.

"You have no idea," he said, his voice husky, his eyes dark.

"Oh really?" I said, sitting down in a chair. I tried to make it casual, but my knees had forgotten how not to buckle when he said that, so it was more out of necessity.

Brent came around his desk. I saw the growth of stubble I'd felt with my palm and fingers, saw that he hadn't been sleeping. This was tearing him up, this breach of ethics that threatened his company. I saw that he couldn't play fast and loose with sexual harassment rules, bend those policies just to get with me. I knew it was too risky, especially with the current legal wrangling hanging over his head. He didn't know if I was an opportunist hoping to blackmail him.

"Brent," I said soberly. "I love the banter, but I need to be serious for a second."

He stood in front of me, leaned against his desk, "Shoot," he said.

"I wouldn't—talk about you. Or anything you said or that we did together. I'm not going to be someone who takes advantage of you that way."

He smiled and nodded. "I'm a grown man. If I take risks, it is because I choose to take them. Of course, you could be a danger to me. You have the power to ruin my reputation, my company if you wanted, but you've given me no indication that you want to destroy anything."

"I don't. I want to fix things. I told you before, I'm a natural at it. I know this is a tenuous time for the company."

"That's very practical of you," he said with a slow grin that made me feel a warm twist in my belly.

"If there's anything I can do to help you," I said, "all you have to do is ask."

"I'm asking."

I felt an almighty thud of my heart, "What are you asking?"

I was gripping the arms of my chair like I was riding Star Tours at Disney and everything was lurching to one side.

"I've been waiting for this," he said, a predatory look on his face, the dark focus of his eyes making me feel uneasy and off-balance.

I stood up. I didn't know what lay ahead for me, but I knew I wasn't going to sit down for it. I straightened the wrap dress I was so proud of, the silk hanging just right and clinging to my curves. I was so glad I'd splurged on it because billionaire Brent Waltham was about to show it a good time by all indications.

He leaned in close, his fingers trailing down my neck just the way I'd imagined. It was easy to feel like he left trails of flames on my skin. My eyes began to drift shut when his whisper stopped me, "No, look at me." My eye met his and held them. It felt like a force rocketed through me when our eyes locked. He slid his hand around the back of my neck beneath my hair. His thumb massaged my scalp. I could have purred from the pleasurable sensation of that alone. My lips parted, wanting his.

"I'm going to walk you over here to this wall beside the door. Up in the corner, a camera is mounted. If we stand beneath it, we won't be recorded," he whispered against my ear. The sensation of his breath on my skin made my toes curl up in my shoes. I nodded.

"Is that alright with you?".

"Yes," I said.

With his hand on my neck, he guided me backward one step at a time until I felt the wall against my back. Brent loomed over me, tall and broad, his body shading me, blocking out the light from the window. He reached out and leaned his hand against the wall beside me. When he slid his palm down beside my face, I shivered because he might as well have run his hand down my spine. I held on to his arm, gripped his bicep below his shoulder, thick and muscular. My pulse beat wildly, and my vision was bright. If he didn't kiss me soon, I thought I might honestly faint.

"I feel like I've wanted this since the minute I laid eyes on you," he said, "after all this time, I won't be rushed."

When Brent grinned at me, the good lines around his

eyes crinkled up and it did things to my lady parts. They clenched and grew wetter. I let my eyes break away from his and slide down his body. I could see the bulge in his trousers, and a smug smile of satisfaction touched my lips just to see the evidence that he was as affected as I was by this pull between us.

"Oh, yes, I feel it. I feel it like knives, Cat. Even in my sleep," he murmured with his lips against my cheekbone.

He kissed my cheek, his thumb still stroking in my hair, soothing me. I felt transfixed by his gaze, his lips. Almost afraid that if I moved at all he might stop touching me.

"Are you scared?" he said, drawing back a little. I shook my head.

"Scared that you'll stop. That this is all I'll ever have," I admitted.

"This isn't all. This is barely the beginning," he promised.

Just as I began to close my eyes again, I made myself meet his gaze. The heat in his eyes made me gasp. He kissed my cheek again. I couldn't wait any longer. I turned toward his mouth like a compass needle swinging helplessly toward the north.

Our lips touched, and we sprang apart instantly.

"Holy hell," he groaned, taking my face in both hands then and tilting it before he pressed his lips to mine again.

That second contact felt as good as the first, as shocking. His lips were soft and strong, rubbing against mine sensuously before our lips locked and clung. I swore because it felt so incredible, and he chuckled in response. Then he pushed his tongue into my mouth, and I swear to God I about blacked out.

"Fuck," he groaned, stroking in again and again. My tongue mated with his, and he pulled me closer into his arms. My head bent back across his arm as we kissed deeply, urgently. His hand slid down my neck to my collarbone, then fanned out across the bare skin above where the top of my dress crossed. The heat of his hand made me arch toward him, pressing up until he was palming my breast, squeezing it. My hand was in his hair. I was moaning right out loud from the fiery sensations on my skin and shooting down to my belly. I writhed in his grip, needing more. I had never known that kissing or making out could be like this, could be hotter than any sex I'd ever had.

My dress was riding up because I had hooked my leg around his. His thumb worked my nipple hard as we kissed breathlessly. I whimpered, ready to beg. He could have had me there, against the wall in his office and I would have pleaded for more. I was that debauched by just his kiss, his slightest touch. When I turned my face just to get a breath, his voracious mouth took my neck, licking and sucking, making bolts of pleasure slither down my body. It was all I could do not to grab for him, not to take his hand and shove it up my dress and say, *feel this, feel how wet you've made me.*

"Brent," I gasped.

He pulled back a little and grinned wickedly, "That's one of the ways I imagined you saying my name, breathless on the end of a moan. There were other ways—against my skin, into my mouth, screaming it into the dark as I took you again and again, making you come until you're helpless."

"Oh, God, Brent," I said, sounding cheesy and horny as I was.

"Yes, Cat. This. This is what we've felt since you touched my hand at the lunch table. That feeling that ran through you, I felt that, too. Like we would fit together perfectly," he said.

He took my mouth again. I reached for his face, turned him so his back was to the wall. He laughed softly against my lips, kissed me harder. Slowly we slid down the wall until he sat on the floor. With his help, I straddled his lap, my dress rucking up around my thighs. I arched back against his knees when he put his mouth to my chest. I was spread out for him like a feast, the heat coiling in my body, knowing I was so wound up that all he would have to do was touch me and I'd go off like fireworks. I rose up on my knees. His big hands slid up my dress and cupped my ass, squeezing it as I kissed him, my hair tumbling in our faces. He stopped to bury his face in my cleavage, to lick and suck there, until I grabbed his face and made him kiss me again, soft, quick bites on my lips until I was dizzy with need. He sucked my bottom lip between his and pulled me into his arms. There was a tremor in his embrace. He was shaking as he kissed me and crushed me against his chest.

I would never be the same after this.

BRENT

I had to go to LA for a few days. As busy as I was, I still replayed my encounter with Cat in my mind probably five times a day. It had been a mistake. Of course, it was. She was a junior employee. I had mauled her against the wall of my office. I'd taken advantage of her whether she thought so or not. I needed to apologize and then see much less of her. I'd tell Millie that the special project was over. I would avoid her if necessary.

I sat in meetings forcing myself not to fantasize about Cat. Once, I looked up thinking I had seen her pass the door. It wasn't her. She was all the way across the country. She was still too close. I couldn't concentrate.

I went from LA to Hawaii for Tom's bachelor party. It was a whole weekend. There was a luau with a pig roasting on a spit and hula dancers and all the rum you could drink. We stayed in a private villa with a view of Diamondhead. We surfed, which was amazing. It was a source of pride for Tom to have found something I'd never done before—a champion surfer gave us lessons. Before long I was going down to the beach at dawn to practice. It felt so good to find that perfect spot where I balanced on the light board and could shift my weight to ride the waves. I wiped out a hundred times, slapped in the face by water as I tumbled off the board. The only time I was truly free of the warring regret and longing over Cat was when I was on the water. Even then, I missed her. I wanted to show her the view, see her try to surf and probably put me to shame at it out of sheer stubbornness.

I wanted to call her. I didn't have her personal number that fact galled me. The only way to get it would be to contact HR at the company because she was an employee. As in, I was screwing around with someone who worked for me. I shook my head, refused to request her number. There were excellent sushi and a superior sake the last night. There were also hula dancers that stripped. Beautiful local dancers who took off their beads and bikini tops and grass skirts and danced. I stared at my sake, checked my email. I felt uncomfortable even looking at them. When I had to look up because Drew elbowed me, I looked at their knees. No strippers' knees had ever been so stared at, knees and feet. A quick glance up and I was able to appear interested while watching their hair and occasionally their hands when they raised them above their heads.

Before long, everyone was up dancing with the strippers. Tom was doing body shots off one of them. Two of the board members, both in their heart attack years, were trying to do the limbo. Drew was twerking on one of the dancers in a way that made me want to whip out my phone and video it because it was hysterically bad. Of course, I didn't because taking video at a bachelor party was a terrible idea. Especially when everyone went into the pool, naked strippers, executives in golf clothes and all. The groom came up with a flower between his teeth which had come off of a stripper

I went and refilled my sake, staying dry. I felt a hand on my shoulder and turned to see a soaking wet, naked stripper behind me.

"We could go back to your room," she suggested with a sly smile. I shook my head.

"No thank you. I think I'm going to turn in now. I doubt they'll notice I'm gone. Have a good evening."

I returned and watched the news in my room, doing some work. When I got a text message, I glanced up. I didn't know the number.

"I've missed you," it said, "this is Cat."

I had forgotten about giving her my private number. I held the phone, read the text over and over. Then I set the phone aside. It had been a mistake. To message her, to call her would be to make things worse so I sulked alone in my room in Hawaii while a wild bachelor party roared downstairs without me.

11

CAT

He was gone for days. Life went on. I worked. I went to yoga class and hung out with friends. I spent too much on a lingerie set in hopes that he'd see it soon. Then I caved and texted him. I had awakened early and was lying there at dawn, missing him so much. He never replied so he was ghosting me. The guy I had such a connection to, my college fantasy guy. He was done with me. I was still going to have to work with him. Admittedly, unless I tried to meet with him, I'd see his face more in the company newsletter than in real life, but it would hurt just the same. I had feelings for him, feelings that went beyond lust. It didn't matter that we hadn't known each other that long. We clicked in every way possible—the effervescent feeling of joy when we talked and teased, the unbelievable way we both reacted to our first kiss. It had seemed like we were meant to be. Until it didn't.

So I went to work that Monday expecting exactly nothing. Instead, I found a latte on my desk with a note from him, asking me to come to his office. I was giddy about it. I rushed to the ladies' room and fixed my lipstick and my hair.

I couldn't wait to see him. The women in the elevator gave me side-eye because I was practically bouncing up and down with excitement. Shrugging, I indicated my latte, "These are so good. I've had NINE today and the caffeine isn't even bothering me," I said with a fake grin while they exchanged a look. Let them talk. I was going to see Brent.

When I reached Millie's desk, she nodded, "Go right in." I thanked her and breezed into his office.

I sailed across the room to greet him. My face was open and beaming at him as I reached for him and watched him take a step back.

"Caitlin," he began.

My full name.

Shit.

"What?" I said, stepping back and taking a seat. This was going to hurt.

"What happened between us was a serious mistake. I deserve all the blame as both the senior staff and your ultimate supervisor."

I tried not to let him see how badly his words stung. "You didn't answer my text, Brent. I got the message. You don't want me. If that's all, I'd like to get back to work."

I got to my feet and threw my latte in his trash untouched. It splattered up on the side of his desk, and I wasn't sorry.

"You ruined a bachelor party for me," he said as I was leaving.

"What? Did my text interrupt your keg stand and make you lose? Or were you licking something off a stripper and the text alert distracted you and you had to start over?"

"I kept thinking of you."

"Then why didn't you say something? Why didn't you respond to my text? I spent the whole weekend thinking about how good you made me fell up against that wall over there."

"I wish you wouldn't say that. This isn't appropriate. I made a serious mistake with you. I apologize, which is something I seldom do, but I was in the wrong, and I have done you harm. I should never have encouraged your interest or said and done the things I did. I take full responsibility for the way I've treated you as a new hire—"

"I don't mind being discreet. If that's the problem," I said. I hated myself so much for saying it, but I also couldn't leave that room without admitting it. Even though it felt craven, like pleading, I also felt strong because of the two of us, I was the only one brave enough to own up to how I felt.

"I like you that much," I added.

Brent shook his head. "You deserve better than that. Better than this. The only answer is for us to see less of one another. Not to see one another at all. I'm sorry, Caitlin. I have done some things in my life that I should have done differently, but I can tell you this, I have never in my life said a harder goodbye than this."

"That's because you're too stubborn to let yourself be happy. You're looking at things on paper, not in real life. And I can tell you *this*, Brent Waltham. I've dreamed of you for years, and I never once believed you were a coward. But you are."

I stormed out and slammed the door. I was hurt, sure, and felt rejected. But I also knew I was right for all the damn good it did me. I would miss him and wish things were different, but he would regret me for the rest of his life. I knew it. Just as surely as I knew that, even when I got over this loss, I'd never have another first kiss like that again. He had, in such a short span of time, ruined men for me.

I would date. I might even find someone and get marrie,

but at night, I'd think of Brent. Something would remind me of him—white wine or an elevator or someone else's smile. And I'd be right back there, falling too hard and fast in love. That was the one thing I hadn't told him as a matter of pride. Maybe in time it would become less true. Less painful.

That night I went out. I wasn't one to wallow. I stayed out until two and even gave my number to the guy I had been dancing with. He had tried to kiss me, but I had shied away. Still, giving him my number had to count as resilience at least a little.

1 2

BRENT

I sat in the cigar lounge at Club Nine Three with Malcolm. I didn't tell him a single word about Cat. I didn't need to. Instead, I smoked two cohibas. I drank far too much, long after Malcolm gave up and went home to his wife and baby. I rode back to the office and slept there in my clothes.

She was wrong. I was no coward, but I was sure as hell lonely. Not just lonely, though. The kind of lonely that only she could satisfy. What I felt for her and with her had been too intense, too strange. Too deeply wrong. I couldn't justify it. I had always been a creature of the mind more than of the heart or the flesh. So when those strong feelings took over, I forced them back into their box. I would not have my life take a drastic wrong turn just for a brief affair, something sordid and ultimately dangerous to my reputation and business. And harmful to her as well, because she was so young and bright and brave, and deserved better than the obsessive interest of an older lonely man who craved her energy and youth and passion. It made me feel like I was a hundred years old and more than a little vampiric. I had to stay clear of her. For her good as well as mine.

The next morning I was up early and ran four miles. I had a conference call about a company I was looking to acquire. Legal contacted me to let me know that the young woman appreciated our support and would accept our first offer without pursuing legal action. "Give her another half million. She deserves more, after the way she was treated," I said gruffly. I hated all of it, especially paying her off.

Maxwell had fled to California. He had been the reason for my trip to LA. His threats of going to the media with information about me had been silenced. Any information he had would have violated his nondisclosure clause and would have landed him in more hot water than he already was. I personally delivered a signed declaration to his professional organization denouncing his criminal activity and demanding that he be expelled. His reputation was in tatters, and his wife had left him. Criminal charges were pending, with which we were cooperating fully. He was being extradited back east for incarceration pending a hearing. It did my heart good to think of him locked up for what he'd done.

I arranged a dinner with the board of directors to celebrate the resolution of the troubling situation. We shut down a popular Italian restaurant for the party. I was pleased to detail the arrangements for them and to show them evidence of our indemnification in the proceedings. Justice would be served, and Astley Corp would thrive.

Alex, the chairman, made a toast to my handling of the situation. I accepted, then toasted our chief legal counsel in turn. I caught them up on the revisions to our training program and policies. Nate tapped his glass, "I move that we table all discussion of business and have an enjoyable evening," he said. "Hear, hear!" they said, charging their glasses.

"All work and no play, Brent," Alex's wife Linda chastised playfully.

"Makes me a rich man, Linda," I returned cheerfully.

"Surely you have enough money and power to take a break, find yourself a wife... or husband," she said, "And settle down."

"I'm afraid the family life is not for me. I'll leave that to the lot of you and all your beautiful families. I'll content myself to be godfather and uncle and buy them all ponies and motorcycles and other things you don't want them to have," I said.

"I'm the first to congratulate you on a job well done," Alex said, "but my wife, as usual, makes an excellent point. You've made a sustainable corporation very successful. You've attained massive wealth for yourself, not to mention the rest of us. How often does a board of directors tell the CEO he should slow down and enjoy life?"

"When they think he's old and should retire?" I suggested.

"No!" three of them protested at once.

"Just cut back a little. You have a COO, a CFO, and plenty of executive VP's who can take some of the workload off of you, give you time to pursue a real life," Nate said.

"I'm going to Tom's wedding next week. You'll all be rid of me for four days. Content yourselves to believing I'm off somewhere pursuing marriage and children instead of on Malcolm's yacht getting a tan and drinking Patrón," I said as dinner was served.

We ate and chatted about their vacations and kids and

home renovations. Linda's Yorkie had done well in a state-level dog show, and I admired photos of it. There was a good deal of looking at people's phones to exclaim over photos of their vacation home, graduating offspring, vintage cars, and large watercrafts. I made sure to make comments and smile at each. I had no photos to display, but I had plenty to be proud of. There was no reason to feel uneasy or left out.

No reason to wish Cat were there with me to make me laugh about which was cuter, the show Yorkie or the old Shelby Mustang. It would've been a different experience with her there, lighter and funnier, somehow easier to take. I liked these people and we had accomplished a great deal together in both commerce and philanthropy. We shared goals and memories. Not one of them knew I'd lost a child. Not one of them had favorite elevators. I shrugged and took a drink. I was a little bruised from my near-miss with Cat Sherman, but there was no reason to let that misguided obsession invade every part of my life.

"Why is it you never bring a date to these dinners?" Linda asked.

"I don't want to share the limelight, obviously," I said, "and where could I find a woman who understands my first loyalty is to Astley."

"We all appreciate how dedicated you are, Brent," Alex said.

"Please don't make a concerned speech about my personal life. I am where I want to be," I said.

We all drank another toast to reaching our goals. I stayed until one, picked up the tab and said good night. I was tired of being positive and tired of acting like I was ecstatically happy. If I didn't feel like my friends knew me well enough, that was my fault for not sharing with them. If I wanted a relationship, I should find someone suitable. If I didn't like sleeping alone, that could be managed as part of the relationship.

I knew all of that rationally, but my body or my gut or something disagreed because I kept remembering Cat—the way her mouth felt against mine, the smell of her hair, and the taste of her kiss. The small shiver that ran through her when our tongues tangled together. The strength in her hands as she clutched my arms. Something in me wouldn't let her go.

And for one night, I'd indulge that memory. Let myself fantasize about what it would have been like to have her. Just once. If I knew it was my only chance.

I let my eyes drift shut and imagined her. In my mind, she was wearing that wrap dress, the one she'd had on the night we kissed in my office. It had been thin and silky, blue and white. She stood framed in my doorway, the light behind her, her hair loose across her shoulders. She'd stride toward the bed and tell me she'd had enough of my fake noble bullshit and we were going to make this right. In bed.

I'd reach for her, find her warm and solid under my hands as I pulled her to me. Her lips would part beneath mine as I rolled her under me. I reached beneath the sheets and took my cock in hand, stroking it, feeling it hot and thick in my grip. I imagined it was her hand as I stroked and pumped, jerking off to the thought of her thighs spread before me, my cock sinking into her at last, thrusting once, twice before coming hard and way too fast inside of her tight, wet passage. I would kiss her and kiss her, pull her against my chest and hold her. I'd finger her, lick her, make her come again and again. I would spend myself inside of her until we both were exhausted and weak from lovemaking. Then I would hold her, would spend a whole night with her in my arms, and then kiss her awake in the morning.

I had never been so restless, so fixated on one woman. I cleaned up and went back to bed, falling asleep to thoughts of her, of my mouth on hers and her arms wound around my neck.

13

CAT

Sarah Jo and Layla were a distraction and a comfort whenever we talked. They knew I'd had a crush on my boss, we'd flirted a little, and that I was sad now. They didn't know we had made out against his office wall or that I had worn out a set of double-A batteries thinking about the man. They didn't know that I missed him so much.

I wanted to text him—all the time—about stupid, hilarious things I saw or thought and knew he'd appreciate and laugh about, but I held myself back. I'd learned my lesson after all. Texting him got me nothing except rejection so I didn't contact him. I didn't see him at all.

For a few days, I moped around. Then when Jason from marketing asked me out for coffee, I said yes. We had lattes and split a piece of buttery coffee cake and talked shit about people who manage to live without carbs. It was fine. There was no spark whatsoever, but he was nice enough. He didn't take my mind off Brent for even five minutes, but I had to start somewhere. Like going out with a nice man who didn't deserve to be compared to a guy who didn't even want me.

So when Jason asked me to go out again, for a real

dinner, I agreed. Then he pissed me off by sending me flowers, a little glass cube of white roses that was waiting on my desk. It was a considerate and romantic gesture completely ruined for me by his name on the card. I wanted them to be from Brent. Some lavish apology that would send me rushing into his office to try out the plush couch in the corner.

I walked over to marketing and thanked Jason for the beautiful flowers. I even said I was looking forward to our dinner. Over lunch, I had an eyebrow waxing appointment and bought a new top to wear on the date. I was going to act like this was something to look forward to. Even if it felt like looking forward to a root canal. Going anywhere with another man felt wrong. It felt like I was being disloyal, unfaithful even. It didn't' matter to my stupid, pathetic heart that Brent Waltham had shown me the door. No, I should be true to him forever. No cute guys from marketing, no flowers or coffee or dinner. I should have just wandered around my apartment, refusing to change out of that wrap dress like some demented Miss Havisham.

It didn't matter that I wanted a full and happy life. And even if Brent wanted nothing more than his career and an unblemished reputation, I wanted more. I wanted a partner, a man who listened to me and laughed with me and kissed me extremely well. A man who'd spoon up behind me in bed and let me put my cold feet on his legs. And Brent Waltham didn't want to be that man. Not even if I'd debase myself by sneaking around with him and pretending in public like we'd only met a couple of times. Like I wasn't already crazy about him.

Jason from marketing was no better off than Blandy had been, even worse in fact. Blandy had only been compared to my Forbes fantasy man, who had been charming when we met. Jason had to stand up to the memory of the sexiest man, the greatest kisser I'd ever known. He was doomed to fail, poor latte-drinking bastard. With his stupid flowers. They were lovely flowers. They were just from the wrong man.

And this was how it was going to end—with me dating a series of wrong men, marrying a wrong man because the right man had reservations about being with me, reservations that were stronger than his feelings for me. Even when nothing was stronger than what I felt for him. He had refused to sneak around and be secret lovers, but I still wanted him in spite of that. In spite of the fact that he didn't choose me. How pathetic. I had to move on.

And moving on meant going out with Jason, just for somewhere to start. I got dressed up. I made myself text Sarah Jo and Layla to tell them how excited I was. I was faking excitement. I might as well get used to that because I'd be faking orgasms soon enough. I sighed. No, I wouldn't fake those. I'd just teach the guy what I liked. I deserved orgasms, even if they were with the wrong man.

14

BRENT

In a week, I'd be on my way to Greece. The travel arrangements were made, all my interim work had been delegated successfully to qualified people. Tom's wedding was looming ahead of me. Instead of a fun break, a chance to spend time with friends in the Greek Isles, I considered it with dread. If I hadn't cared so much for Tom, I would have canceled. He was part of my inner circle. He was a brother. For a brother, I could endure this for a few days. The celebration of a new beginning for a couple in love. I could even put aside the recollection I had of Tom jumping in the pool with the strippers in Hawaii.

Briefly, I considered inviting a date to the wedding. It would make me feel better, perhaps. Except there was no one I could invite who would feel like a partner in crime, there to celebrate but also make soothing sarcastic comments during the toasts at the reception. No one but Cat. Cat, who I had kissed a few times in my office. Cat, who was far too young and an employee. Cat, who felt like the only person who really spoke the same language I did. She was the person I wanted by my side at that absurd,

86

decadent wedding celebration. I couldn't ask her after the way I'd treated her. And the objections I'd had to a relationship with her remained valid. It was unethical, improper, unfair to her.

Sifting through my emails and jotting down notes, I looked up when Millie entered my office.

"Brent, sorry to interrupt. Is your off-the-books special project with the girl from HR completed?"

"Yes, why?" I said.

"I'm removing her from the carte blanche list then. In case I ever take a sick day, I keep that sort of information up to date for whatever poor bastard you get to take my place," she said wryly.

"You may remove her from the list, thank you."

She continued to stand in the doorway.

"Anything else?" I inquired.

"Are there plans to update the policy on interoffice dating as well as harassment? Because Little Miss HR is seeing Jason from Marketing."

The news left a bitter taste on my tongue. "Aren't you just a well of information," I said sarcastically.

"My ability to discover this sort of information is one of the reasons you gave me a raise, Brent," she said.

"Agreed. I do like to know what's going on in my building. However, as it relates to Ms. Sherman, I don't wish to be informed. Unless there is some harassment allegation; it is none of my concern at all," I said decisively.

"I see. And if she comes here wanting to see you?"

"She's off the list, Millie. I'm sure she knows how email works," I said a little sharply.

"She must have made quite an impression on you," Millie said.

"Sometimes you're too observant for your own good," I said ruefully.

She turned to leave.

"Millie—if she shows up, send her in," I said, defeated.

"I thought so. Just making sure," she said with her infuriating smile.

I was glad she was on my side. Because Millie would be a formidable enemy, I thought for probably the hundredth time. She was observant and that was very valuable to me. It was just irritating when she noticed things about me that I would rather think were discreet. Like the lingering feelings I harbored for Caitlin.

15

CAT

Steadying myself on a kitchen chair, I wondered if the tree pose counted when you had to hold on to something. The woman in the video seemed so relaxed while she stood on one foot. I moved through the poses in the routine and breathed when they told me to. I had been doing yoga classes every day at the gym, but I just didn't want to see people for once.

So I did my YouTube yoga and took a shower. I shaved my legs as if I were hopeful. I wasn't hopeful. First off, I had no intention of sleeping with anyone before date six at the earliest. Secondly, unless Jason turned out to be a lot more interesting than I initially found him, there would be no date six or even date three. I couldn't even make myself imagine kissing him. Not holding his hand.

I felt vaguely sorry for Jason and anyone who happened to come after Brent, because with nothing more than a lunch and some flirting kisses, Brent had set the bar way too high for anyone to compare. Jason didn't have much of a chance. But still, I curled my eyelashes and put on two coats of mascara. I figured the first step in getting over rejection was to act like I was fine. If I looked dressed up and excited, maybe I could fool myself. One of these days, I'd look in the mirror, and I wouldn't have to pretend to smile anymore. One of these days, it would be real.

In the meantime, I looked around, wondering why I kept forgetting to bring those flowers home. They were still on my desk. Jason had been nice enough to send me a bouquet, and I had just left it at work. Looking in my mirror told the whole story because there, tucked right in the corner of the mirror, was Brent Waltham's business card. He had pushed it across the lunch table toward me with one finger, and I'd taken it. I'd stowed it safely in my purse so I didn't lose it, and I had brought it right home and stuck it on my mirror that way it wouldn't get lost.

Maybe I had even traced the embossed letters of his name with my fingertip a few times while willing him to call me or text me or send a carrier pigeon with a message. I still kept it right there. His card. His name and personal number. Not that I would call it or text it again. I had learned my lesson. Or had I? Because his card was still on my mirror.

If I had so much as considered bringing Jason back to my apartment, wouldn't I have taken that card down and put it in a drawer? Or better yet, in the trash can? Exactly. No intention of pursuing a serious relationship with Jason or anyone else, just me and my business card for life. I rolled my eyes, pinched the card between two fingers and plucked it from the mirror. I tossed it in a drawer. I couldn't throw it away yet, but at least it would be out of sight.

In a fit of brokenhearted rage, I had ripped up my old copy of Forbes. It was gone. No more afternoon delight with Brent's handsome face partly in shadow. I couldn't sleep with it in my apartment. It should have been gone long ago, with my One Direction poster and my crush on Harry Styles, so the magazine was out of my life just like the man himself.

I put on more lipstick. I stepped into my kitten heels and answered the door when Jason rang the bell.

He brought flowers. Of course, he did. Because the only thing wrong with him was the incontrovertible fact that he wasn't Brent. I thanked him for the flowers, put them in a vase and told him they were beautiful. The typical protocol.

"You're spoiling me," I said, trying a little bit to be coquettish.

"I've been looking for someone to spoil for a while now. I like making you happy," he said.

Shit. Not only was he not Brent, but he was also too good for me. I felt bad for him. I wanted to clap him on the shoulder and say, *dude, there's someone out there for you, but it isn't me. Don't waste your flowers on a woman who's in love with someone else.* Instead, I grabbed a coat and thanked him when he told me how nice I looked.

"You look great, too," I said.

And he did look great. He had nice sandy blond hair and cute wire-rimmed glasses. His fingernails were clean, and he had good teeth. What else could a woman want in a man? He wasn't crude or an obvious racist or anything that should be a turn off for me. And yet there we were, taking an Uber to the new Greek place he'd heard about, smiling blandly and commenting on the weather.

"It *is* getting colder," I said encouragingly like I was his kindergarten teacher as if I was ensuring him that he did know what sound the letter 'b' makes.

"Pretty soon I'll have to break out my winter climbing gear," he said.

"Oh, you climb?"

"Yeah. I love it. I've been rock climbing since I was ten."

"Great. Do you go to a gym or what?"

"I like to climb outside. I have a few favorite spots. I could show you one," he offered.

"I'm more of a yoga girl myself," I said. It wasn't his fault that I didn't like outdoor sports or heights or the idea of crime scene tape around my body after I was maybe pushed off a cliff for having a smart mouth.

"Really? I haven't done yoga. Isn't it just stretching?"

"Actually, it's a martial art that combines breathing and concentration exercises with a series of poses to increase flexibility and strength," I said, "It helps me de-stress so I don't eat all the Hostess cupcakes ever made."

"Right. So, climbing does that for me. Not the cupcakes thing, but the stress reduction. Just being out in nature and pushing my body to its limits. It relaxes me and puts me in the moment."

"That's great," I said, wondering what to talk about as we lulled into an awkward silence.

The restaurant was good. He offered me a spanakopita, and I accepted it to be polite and ate it. It was crisp and tasty. After we discussed our travels (I hadn't been out of the country, he had been to Mexico with friends), we talked a little about food. He thought black bean burgers were as good as the real thing. I nodded. I said I liked Eggs Benedict. He nodded. Then we stopped talking and ate. It wasn't excruciating, but it wasn't fun either. We didn't have an easy rhythm or a rapport. There was nothing we could make into an inside joke that we had in common. When he suggested dessert, I lied and said I was stuffed just because I was tired of spending time with him, and bored of him trying to make it fun.

He had the Uber stop at my apartment building and

clearly waited to be asked up. I shook my head, said I had a nice time, but that I wanted to turn in early. He leaned over to kiss me goodnight, but I shied away. I almost apologized, but there was no reason to. We didn't click. There was no chemistry. It wasn't anyone's fault. I just waved from the door, and the Uber drove off with him inside it.

Sarah Jo texted to see how my date went an hour later. I told her I was already home, and it was a bust. There was nothing wrong with him, just no spark. She suggested I go to the botanical gardens or a park the next day because for Sarah Jo, plants were the next best thing to taking care of everyone. I told her I'd think about it. I didn't mention that outdoors isn't my jam. I'd much prefer looking at animal rescue web sites so I could start choosing cats for my future as a crazy cat lady.

That's what I would do. Find a cat. Not waste time regretting the Forbes magazine I'd thrown away. See, I had a plan.

16

BRENT

Before facing the wedding, I had to run what felt like a gauntlet of social obligations. One night was a charity function at a museum. The next was a trip to the opera as a favor to Harold, one of the directors on Astley's board. His newly divorced daughter was in town, and he had gotten her tickets to the opera. He thought she'd enjoy it more if I took her than if she had to go with him. I had agreed and even acted pleased about it. I could show an out-of-towner how beautiful and cultured our city was and enjoy the opera.

No one enjoys opera. People may pretend to enjoy it so they seem smart or else they understand German and Italian better than I do. Either way, I'd attended just enough productions to know I didn't like it. So a set-up date with a recent divorcee to attend an activity I didn't like wasn't a promising obligation. But I had agreed to it, so I put on my Armani tuxedo and squired Ella from her hotel to dinner and then the opera house.

At the opera, she started to cry, but not because of the

long and boring production. Apparently, the real reason she was crying was because it dawned on her that she's thirty-eight years old and starting over, divorced. And also ma because she couldn't hold her wine. I offered to get her a bottle of water, but she declined. She accepted my handker-chief, blew her nose and then went to the ladies' room to 'fix her face.' I sat staring at the performers, wishing Cat was there to make fun of it with me. She would have had me cracking up with fake dialogue for the actors, I knew. Admonishing myself for obsessing, I went to the lobby to see if Ella wanted to give up on the opera. She emerged with fresh makeup on and swore she loved the opera and wouldn't dream of missing it. Back we went to our seats and another hour and a half of loud foreign singing passed.

I stayed awake. I nodded and agreed with all of her remarks. I was counting down until I could take her back to her hotel and leave her there. In the car, she asked if I wanted to go up to her room for a drink. I shook my head.

"I'm flattered, and I hope you've had a good evening. I'm just not in a place to get serious with anyone, and you deserve a man who is."

"It wouldn't have to be serious," she said, biting her lip.

I kissed her cheek, "Ella, have a Merry Christmas, and I wish you the best in the new year. You deserve so much better."

She finally nodded and said good night. On the way back to my place, I texted Cat.

I didn't know why I finally broke down and did it. Perhaps it was my evening with Ella. Perhaps it was the upcoming wedding and the knowledge that I had no one who really knew me. Or it could be that I missed her for who she was, her voice and her humor and her energy.

After I hit send, I wondered if I was making a mistake. I knew I was, but I also knew it could be a mistake of the most delicious kind.

CAT

I was watching a documentary about a serial killer and searching for rescue cats online, which sounds creepier than it was. I paused to fish for a piece of popcorn I'd dropped down the front of my pajama top when my phone buzzed.

I looked down to see Brent's name flash across my screen.

I sat down and held my phone in my hands. It lit up again with, "I know it's late. Would you go out for a drink with me?"

A drink sounded legit like he wanted to talk. Not like he was drunk and wanted to bone someone convenient. I looked at myself and decided that going out wasn't something that would take less than an hour to get ready for. So I decided to play it cool for once.

Nah, it's late. In my pj's. You could come over for ice cream if you can find me in the slums, I texted, joking. My cute apartment was far from the slums, but nowhere near his tax bracket.

Send me your address.

I sent him my location and waited. And by waited, I meant that I picked up stuff, cleared off the coffee table, and put on a pushup bra under my striped pajamas. I curled my lashes and put on mascara—not enough makeup to be obvious but enough to keep me from looking completely unappealing.

When he knocked at the door, I composed myself and took a deep breath and smiled before I opened it. I stepped back to let him in. I didn't go into his arms to be crushed in a hug I needed so badly. I felt diffident and shy, wanting to be sure this wasn't just another step forward into two steps back.

We sat down at my kitchen table and dished chocolate chip ice cream into my deep, blue bowls. I took a bite.

"Why did you text me? And why were you at the opera? Did you lose a bet?""I was doing a favor for a friend. You know Harold Street?"

"I know the name. Industrialist, retired, lots of shipping I think."

"That's the one. He's on the board of directors, a seat he earned by having his shipping empire acquired by Astley seven years ago."

"So he took you to the opera?"

"No. I had to take his daughter to the opera. She's divorced, in town for the holidays or something."

"Couldn't you take her to do something fun?"

"Harold gave her tickets to this."

"Was he trying to get rid of them?" I said.

"I don't know. She seemed to like it. Maybe it's like casseroles—if you grow up with it, you think it's normal. It could be that way with opera. I would rather have a tater tot casserole any day."

"You and me both. All that yelling. And the woman always dies."

"That's a generalization. Surely the woman doesn't always die," he said.

"Name one opera where she doesn't."

"Marriage of Figaro. Next?"

"Okay, fine. Opera is boring. It's only fun if you pretend they're cats who are yowling because they're really mad about, like, the wrong kind of cat kibble."

"That would have improved this a lot. I wish you'd been there," he said.

"So what brings you here?"

"I miss you."

"You told me to leave you alone."

"I was right. Everyone would be better off if we spent less time together. The only problem is that it makes me miserable because you're the one person I can talk to."

"You have friends to talk to."

"Yes and no. Malcolm is my oldest friend, but he's married to his third wife, has a baby. His perspective is different."

"You prefer the perspective of a twenty-four-year-old junior employee?" I challenged, not ready to let him off the hook.

"I prefer *your* perspective, *your* intelligence, and *your* humor," he said, "I find that I can't let go of the idea of you, of your energy and laughter and the way you see things. So if I'm going to obsess over you, there's not much sense in avoiding you. That is if you can forgive me being self-right-eous and sending you away before, and also being greedy enough to want you back."

"That depends," I said.

"On what exactly?"

"I have no idea, but it sounded more dignified than just saying yes. So I have to come up with some kind of condition. Like I'll only have you back if you, fuck, God, I'm terrible at playing hard to get," I said. "I had a date with Jason from Marketing."

"I know. Millie told me. Just to torment me, I believe. Or else to spur me into action."

"Did you think I was trying to make you jealous? I'm just trying to move on."

"Did you let him kiss you?" he said, his eyes going dark, predatory.

"No," I said, pulse kicking up sharply.

"Will you let me kiss you?" he said.

I nodded, eager as anything, "Yes. I will. That's my condition. You owe me a condition so I'll only have you back if you kiss me. I mean, really kiss me so I never forget it."

"That's the easiest condition ever. All I've wanted to do since you opened that door is kiss you. Come here," he said.

I swear I batted my eyelashes at him. Then I sidled toward him. He opened his knees and I stepped between them. His hands, those big hands I'd fantasized about, were on my hips, pulling me closer. I bent my head toward his, my hands on his face. The scrape of his stubble against my palms, the way the planes of his face felt under my fingers—I almost melted, not being able to believe I had him here. He pulled me onto his lap in a quick motion and slid his hand into my hair. He tilted my face the way he wanted it. Then I opened for him and everything was on fire. Everything in my body was saying *yes*.

He gave me a slow, teasing kiss that ratcheted up my desire until my body hummed, my breathing nothing more than a continual gasp. He had gathered me against his chest, holding me close, and he was working that tongue in my mouth so good that my stomach clenched. Then he pulled away, his hand smoothing across my belly as if he knew how I was reacting.

I stood up and held out my hand. He took it and followed me to my couch. I wasn't ready to trust his return, and definitely wasn't ready to take this to bed. It was too new, too fragile, and exciting. He ran his thumb across my knuckles with a knowing smile as our eyes met. He lifted my hand and kissed it, "Lovely," was all he said.

Brent sat down on the couch beside me. He took my hand, which he was still holding, and laid it against his cheek. He turned his head and kissed my wrist. He slid my loose sleeve back to my elbow and kissed his way up the length of my forearm, just his hot mouth on bare, sensitive skin that had never been kissed before. I felt dizzy like it could be a dream.

"Are you really here?" I whispered.

"This is the only place I want to be, Cat. Here with you. I tried to fight it and be a better man than I am, but I failed so I'm here because I want to kiss you anywhere you'll let me, for as long as you'll have me."

A shudder ran through me at those words. I knew exactly what he meant. I knew if I had whipped off my striped pajama pants, he would bury his face between my legs and lick me there, just the way I'd fantasized about.

"I just thought of another condition. I need a new copy of your Forbes cover," I said.

"Why?"

"I threw mine out."

"I deserved that, but why do you need a magazine cover when you have me?" he said, puzzled.

"You're a busy man. You're not always here, Brent. Sometimes I'm going to need to get off thinking of you."

"I'd give you anything," he said, and seemed to mean it.

"Kiss me," I said.

He cupped my face in his hand gently, stroked my cheekbone with his thumb as he lowered his lips to mine. He was so gorgeous, so incredibly handsome, and his eyes dark and lustful. I felt the quiver of arousal in my belly as I reached for him. We kissed softly back and forth, his tongue trailing along my lower lip, flicking at the roof of my mouth. Then when I was breathless, he pulled me onto his lap, tugged me forward against him so my thighs were around him.

"This is the most fun my couch has ever had," I said with a laugh.

"None of my furniture has had such an evening."

"Not even the bed?"

"I never bring a woman to my bed."

"So no one enters the inner sanctum? Should I make that my goal?"

"If you like," he said, his mouth on my neck.

Brent's hand on my back, his hand on my neck supported me as I arched in his arms. I draped my hands over his shoulders and rose on my knees to kiss him. I gave him deep strokes of my tongue, really tasting him, exploring his mouth and making sure he knew he was mine. I didn't let myself think about loving him, about how much I felt for him or the risks I was taking with my heart. I just kissed him for the sheer physical pleasure of being kissed by a master, of having my body stroked and cradled by a man who knew what to do with his hands.

I had his tuxedo bow tie off and flung it somewhere over his shoulder. I started on his buttons, opening the front of his crisp shirt to get my hands in there on his hot, smooth skin. I kissed his chin, his neck as I felt his arousal growing against my belly. I put my mouth to his chest, tasting that skin, touching the coarse chest hair. I took his hand that was on my hip and ran it up my stomach to my chest. I needed his hands on me, just for a moment, just for relief. I released his hand, and he went after my breast immediately, as if he'd been starved for contact. Kneading, rubbing, giving me the heat and pressure of his touch, squeezing and reveling in my breasts. His thumb worked back and forth over my nipple until I felt heat pooling between my legs. I could have taken him right then, all of him bare, easily because he had me so wet. Still, I had the sense to hold back. To know that it was too soon to give him everything, although I was already his to command. I swallowed the words of love I wanted to say and just ground against him, relishing his hands molding to my body.

Brent kissed me again and again, nipping at my lips and my face, my throat. He pressed a big hand to the small of my back to bring me in contact with his erection, so stiff and thick I thought it impossible. He had a huge cock, and he wanted to put it in me. I wanted him to, wanted it beyond even being able to speak, but I knew it wasn't the time.

Brent shifted me off of his lap and held me against him, so my cheek rested on his chest. I nearly wept at the sensation. I had wanted it so long, this cherishing, this chest and these protective arms, the feeling of being pressed and held to his heart. It made me ache with a beautiful, bittersweet joy. I clutched his shirt and tipped my face up to meet his eyes.

That was when he kissed me, the sweetest, most reverent kiss I'd ever had. Our lips locked, the tip of his tongue lapped at me a little. I moved deeper into the kiss, so he went deeper, tonguing me until I trembled in his arms. He trailed his fingers along my cheek and gave me such a romantic kiss that when our eyes met, he kissed my forehead and hugged me. It was a perfect ending. Then he snuggled me in his arms and rested his cheek on my hair.

"I'm the only one who knows how to kiss you like that," he said a little smugly.

"I'm the only one who makes you want to," I returned.

"You're right," he admitted, "kissing doesn't feel like that with anyone else. It never has."

"And it never will."

"I want you. I've never in my life wanted anyone the way I want you, Caitlyn. Body and soul. It's foreign territory to me. I want to know your thoughts on everything. I want to text you a dozen times a day about something I saw or heard or thought, just to know what you'd say about it. I crave all of you, your mind, your laugh, not only your body. Despite the fact that I'm probably older than your parents."

"You are. But a little gray in the beard is sexy—you should grow this scruff out. It's nice," I said, scratching at his jaw.

"A beard? I've never considered it. In business negotiations, being clean-shaven is usually advantageous as you appear to have nothing to hide."

"But a beard would feel good to me," I said, snuggling up to him.

"A beard it is," he said lightly, "Will it make me look older?"

"Are you that vain? You look like you're too attractive to make movies because you'd distract from all the other actors. You do not need to worry about looking older," I said.

"I hear you. And you're hilarious. Your southern accent

comes out when you get wound up like that," he said indulgently, kissing just below my ear.

"If you keep going, I might just shout yee-haw!" I teased. He laughed. I loved his laugh, loved having him at my house, on my couch, all over me.

"You're beautiful and funny and caring and so sharp, so witty. I can't resist you. I'm done with trying to resist you. I wasn't equipped with the skills to keep from being drawn to you. You're magnetic, Cat. Being around you is preferable to being away from you, but I can't seem to get close enough. It seems there's no solution here," he said, perfectly silly. I kissed him.

"I think you need to go. You sound a little drunk, and I know I'm too happy to be sensible. So tell me good night, and we'll talk tomorrow."

"I'd love to talk to you tomorrow, but I hate to leave you. I could stay in your guest room just to be near you."

"That's a terrible idea. We'd be naked in less than two minutes. Also, I don't have a guest room. This is a one-bedroom so go home before I do something I'll regret," I laughed, but I was a little nervous. If he pressed me, if he coaxed, I was afraid I'd give in because I wanted him, but I wasn't ready to believe he'd really come back to me yet. I needed for this to be real, to last for a little while before I could trust it.

"Good night, then, Cat," he said, and kissed me good night. It was just as devastating as his other kisses, but he kept his word and got up to show himself out, "I'll call you in the morning before I go running."

Then he left and I went to sleep with a smile on my face. On the couch. Because the pillows smelled faintly of his cologne.

18

BRENT

After my run, I called her, even before I showered Just to hear her voice. I was besotted. Stretching out my hamstrings while holding my phone, sweaty and infatuated and hanging on her every word. Malcolm would have laughed his smug ass off at me. Come to think of it, Tom and Drew would have as well.

I felt like I'd been cracked open like I'd been living in a shell, one of those ugly, resin-coated dinosaur eggs from the museum. And then light entered and I reached out toward it and was free. It was the stupidest, goofiest Hallmark feeling. I was embarrassed to admit it to myself. She brought me to life that was what it was. I'd been working, making money, making a difference, but not really living. Not sharing my passions and observations with someone who appreciated them or laughed about them, made them real. Her kiss made everything real.

In the intervening weeks, I'd convinced myself that kissing her in my office had been intense because of the buildup, the sexual tension. It wasn't anything to do with some physical compatibility or New Age soul mates crap.

It was nothing more than the release of all the pent-up desire.

Yet, I was completely wrong because kissing her in her apartment on a kitchen chair meant more to me physically and emotionally than anything in my life. It wasn't posed or photogenic or anything that belonged on the silver screen. It was real and fierce and it was home to me. Holding the armful of Cat on my lap, the delicious size and shape of her, the heft of her on my legs, just the privilege of holding her and kissing her had astonished me. When she led me to the couch she rewarded me with an undeserving kiss. Taking into consideration the way I treated her, I deserved a goodbye or scolding at best. She made me feel like I'd won some magnificent prize. I'd been granted mercy I didn't earn. And I had kissed her hand. She had let me.

Generously, she had spread her legs across my lap and settled on top of me and we had kissed. She had left me breathless, holding her as if I held on for dear life. Nothing could compare to sliding my tongue in her mouth, the power and pleasure of that sensation. As she placed her hands in my hair, on my chest, at my jaw as she suggested I grow a beard—I wanted her so much, felt so connected to her and commanded by her that I would've agreed to paint my nails if she had asked for it.

I would call her, possibly see her. When she answered and said, "Hello there, Brent Waltham," I grinned. I loved it when she said my name.

"Cat."

"Back from your run?" she yawned. It made me long to stretch out in bed beside her.

"Yes. I didn't wait to call. I dialed you as soon as I got back to my driveway."

"You have a driveway? Like a private one? Shut up. You

are rich."

"I realize that. Do you have plans today?"

"Laundry. I have to go to the Laundromat. How about you? More exercise? Millions to make? A beard to grow?" she teased.

"I have more than a driveway. I have laundry facilities. You could do your laundry here, or my housekeeper could do it."

"Are you kidding? Do I want to do my laundry at a fabulous, clean house instead of pumping dollars into a mildewed public machine? Yes, I do, but I don't want to take advantage."

"Really? I'm fairly certain since most of my clothes are dry cleaned, you won't be disturbing anyone."

"For real?" she asked.

I couldn't help but laugh. "Yes, for real. I'll send a car for you, Cat. Give me half an hour to get cleaned up."

"I'll be ready," she said.

I had intended to offer to make her brunch, but I had bribed her with laundry facilities. Very romantic. I jogged up the steep driveway and inside to take my shower. Then I got in one of my cars and drove to her apartment. I messaged to let her know her car had arrived.

She laughed when she saw me, "Moonlighting as a chauffeur?"

"No, I just couldn't wait to see you," I admitted. I loaded her bags into the back and opened her door. Then I leaned in and kissed her lightly. The promise of a whole day together lay before me, and I didn't have the slightest urge to drop her off early and go to the office.

"So I know you don't take women to your home. Do I get to see your house?"

"No, I thought I'd leave you in the car. My housekeeper

will do your laundry and bring it out to you when it's done. Don't worry, I'll leave a window cracked so you get air."

She laughed, that crack of hilarity that seemed to echo in the car, loud and genuine. I took her hand and kissed it as I drove.

"Thank you for that," I said, "For your laugh."

"You better not be serious. I am not sitting in this car all day. I want to go in and dig through the drawers and peek in the closets. Find out all your secrets."

"I got you something," I said, "It's in that bag on the floor."

She reached for the gift bag and pulled out an issue of Forbes with my face on it.

"This isn't the same one."

"No, it's next month's issue. They sent me proofs."

"Shut up. You're doing another cover? Wait, I want the old one, too."

"I'm sure we have loads of them at the office down in archives. I just don't know why you want it."

"I enjoy the articles," she said.

"But you got rid of it. You must have no longer enjoyed those articles," I teased.

"I was pissed at you. I didn't want to look at your stupid, handsome face. Now I do. A girl can change her mind."

"So, how do you feel about relaxing in the hot tub while your laundry is washing?" I said.

"Wait, what? You have your own hot tub?" she said, then laughed, "Loads of people where I come from have a hot tub on their back patio. Now, a lot of them don't heat up anymore, but that doesn't stop anybody."

"Are you saying you're not impressed?"

"I'm saying while yours is probably nicer than the ones I've seen, it's still basically a plug-in bathtub which takes a certain amount of courage anyway because electricity and bathtubs don't work well together."

"I'll have to see how you feel about mine. Unless you're not a water person."

"I'm not an outside person, really. I like pretty views, and when it's hot, I like to get in the water and cool off, but I generally don't like to be uncomfortable. I don't like to be hot or cold or bitten by bugs."

"I see. So you don't want to go for a six-mile run in the mornings?"

"No. I like yoga. And I don't mean posing on a mountaintop yoga-like in the videos. I mean living room yoga," she said, "So don't get any ideas about, hey, let's go do yoga on a volcano."

I laughed, "I didn't say I had a volcano."

"You probably have five."

"I can honestly say I do not own a volcano. Arguably my island in the South Pacific is an atoll with a lagoon at the center and may have once been part of volcanic activity..."

"Told you. You own a volcano or five. What will I even get you for your birthday? Like, a Slinky? Because you have an island. It's not like you'll be, oh cool, a gift card to the movies!"

"A gift card won't be necessary," I said, "I can think of other things, gifts from the heart."

"Oh God. You want me to like rub garlic butter all over myself or something, don't you?" she laughed.

I laughed so hard at the image that it was difficult to drive.

"No. Not garlic butter. In fact, no, I don't find it necessary that you slather edibles on yourself. You're flawless just as you are. I find it difficult to believe my own good luck that you've agreed to spend the day with me."

"It was the washer and dryer that really put you over the top. See, you don't have to entice me with islands or hot tubs. All you need is a laundry room."

"So the key to romance here is not flowers or diamonds, but fabric softener?" I teased.

"I am surprised you even know what that is. Unless you special order yours from the Himalayas so it will be as soft as their goats or something."

"I had a day job and a third-floor walkup in a building with a permanently out of order elevator before I launched my company."

"And you walked uphill both ways?" she laughed.

We turned to go out of the city and then hooked right onto a private drive. I used my fob to open the automated gates. They swung apart, and we drove up the tree-lined path to my house.

"So, got your own yard?" she deadpanned.

"Yes, dirt and grass and everything."

"Nice," she said.

For a man who spent most of his waking hours at the office, I took pride in my home. I'd purchased the Italianate villa in desperate need of renovation. I'd redone it to my own taste, not a designer's. Though I'd lived in a number of high-end properties, including the penthouse in the heart of downtown, this was the first and only place that had felt like home to me since I'd moved out of my grandmother's house at sixteen. I found myself wanting to show it off to Cat in particular.

"I got the place at auction and renovated it about five years ago," I said.

"It's beautiful," she said dutifully.

"If you'll drop your laundry bags by the door, they'll be taken care of."

"No, wait, I want to do them myself," she protested.

"Really? I assure you my housekeeper is perfectly skilled in the care of fine fabrics and is unlikely to damage your clothing."

"It's not that. I don't want somebody to wait on me. I don't mind doing it. It's a treat to get to use a machine without waiting. Really."

"Okay," I said and showed her to the laundry room.

"This place is insane," she said, "I have serious laundry envy."

She studied the electronic panel for a minute and then started her first load, "Thank you," she said sweetly.

"You're welcome," I told her, "would you like to see the rest of the house?"

"I want to see this hot tub, see if it's up to my standards," she joked.

I took her back out to the living room and out the French doors to the back garden. It was chilly, of course, but steam twisted off the surface of the hot tub's shimmering water. She ignored the infinity pool completely and went straight for the huge, square jacuzzi with its natural stone surround and low, rippling waterfall. Cat bent down and dipped her fingers in the water.

"Oh, that is heaven!" she said, looking up at me with a grin. "I want to get in. I don't exactly have my bathing suit though..." she seemed to consider it.

"I think I have a few extras in the pool house from gatherings. You're welcome to see if anything is to your liking."

She regarded me for a moment. "Are you sure?"

"Of course," I said, "You can change in the pool house if you like, or there's a restroom just across from the kitchen."

"Thanks," she said and bounded off excitedly.

I changed into swim trunks and met her out at the hot

tub. She had on a stylish two-piece that showed off her curves in a way that made my mouth water. I held up the chilled bottle of champagne and two glasses that I'd brought.

"Shut up. This is like being on the Bachelor!" she laughed, "No lie, I love that stupid show. Every single season I think they're really gonna find love. Do not fire me for being stupid."

"Let's clear this up. You're not here as an employee of Astley Corp. You're my guest. I asked you to spend the day with me, not with the CEO at your job."

"So nothing I say can be held against me?" she teased.

"Exactly," I said, "we're off the record."

"Good. Now pop the champagne. I'm freezing cold, and you better not get between me and that hot water!"

I stopped unwrapping the top of the bottle because I was distracted by the sight of Cat stepping into the hot tub, sliding down as the water enveloped her and giving a happy sigh. Her sigh ran through me like an electrical shock. My body always responded to her, but that soft, satisfied noise she made had me hard in an instant. I opened the champagne and poured her a glass. Once I was in the hot tub with her, the steam rising off our skin, we toasted to a stolen afternoon. A toast to total privacy and time together.

"So, do you use this a lot?" she said.

"Not as much as I'd like. I swim laps in the pool, but I seldom get in the whirlpool here."

"Why the hell not? I mean, what could be so important that you skip this? I'd be like, hell, sell off three or four companies so I got time to soak!" she laughed. I laughed with her.

"Why sell them? Why not hire people to manage them?" I said.

"How would I know? I don't own companies. And you have lots of hired people but you don't take the time to enjoy what you have. What's that about?" she said. She was looking at me very seriously as she drained her champagne glass.

"I think it's a case of priorities," I said, "I spend most of my time at work because I choose to."

"Why? Do you love working in an office that much?"

"Not really. I like what I can accomplish."

"But you accomplished this. Look around you," she said, gesturing with her empty glass to the beautiful grounds and my home.

I looked at it all just as she suggested. It looked the same as always. I didn't see it with new eyes and suddenly decide to do more self-care or whatever the trending term was, but I liked what I saw, mainly the sight of Cat in my hot tub, indignant and waving a champagne flute.

"If this were an old movie, I'd say it's because I never had anyone to share it with," I said offhandedly.

"Uh, if this were an old movie, we wouldn't be day drinking in a hot tub," she said with a light laugh. I smiled. I couldn't help smiling around Cat. I refilled her glass. She set it on the stone edge of the whirlpool and stretched out her legs, pointing her toes into the waterfall. Her head tipped back and eyes shut, she looked the perfect picture of relaxation.

I thought about edging closer to her on the bench while her eyes were shut, but that was too timid for my taste. I reached out and touched her arm. She turned to look at me.

"Come closer," I said. She grinned at me and cut across the corner of the hot tub to scoot in beside me. I looped my arm around her. She leaned her head on my shoulder and gave another happy sigh.

"This is the best," she said.

I took a drink of champagne and offered her my glass. She took a sip. I liked that, the way she drank from my glass. We sat back and relaxed for a minute.

"I love this. You know what, when I was in eighth grade, I stole my mom's bikini and went and got in a hot tub with Sarah Jo's big brother Ryan."

"Does your friend know you were hot-tubbing with her brother?"

"It wasn't even their hot tub. Or ours. It was a neighbor's," she laughed, "There was this family that moved back north and left their hot tub, the house was empty—we just went out there and plugged it in. He was such a creep too."

"So what you're saying is I'm excellent company as far as men you've been in hot tubs with," I said.

"Exactly. I mean my best friend's brother did try to feel me up—he was sixteen, I was almost fourteen but flat as a board. I had stuffed the top of the bikini so he got a handful of soggy tissues."

"Because you thought stuffing it with tissues and getting wet wouldn't be a problem?" I said dubiously.

"Hey, I didn't say I was smart. I was a late bloomer and none too bright at thirteen either."

"I hope the little creep learned his lesson," I said.

"Oh, I'm not sure he knew the difference. He didn't act like he knew anything was off, so it was probably the first time he ever tried to get to second base."

"I can't say I have a high opinion of your friend's brother since he took an eighth-grader out to an abandoned hot tub to feel her up."

"Hey, it's what passes for romance where I come from," she laughed.

"Really. So how do champagne and laundry facilities rank?"

"Even better than soggy tissues and septic chlorine," she said, "Five stars."

I kissed her then. She wound her arms around my neck and kissed me back. For a time, there was nothing but the churning hot water around us and my mouth on hers. Then she nestled against me, and I held her close, as close as we could be. I pulled her onto my lap. She wrapped her legs around me. I pressed her in my arms and kissed her, my tongue stroking hers, wanting to mark her and make her mine. My hands almost covered her back, and it made me feel strong and powerful. I could almost pull her into me, absorb her. The sensation was intoxicating. She was intoxicating.

"Mr. Waltham? Pardon me, Mr. Waltham?" a voice called from the French doors.

I dragged my mouth from Cat's, reluctant and growing furious. My housekeeper stood with her hands on her hips.

"Forgive me, but the load of washing is done. Do you want these things hung to dry or put in the dryer?" she called.

I made myself take a deep breath. I reminded myself that Clara was an excellent housekeeper. That she managed the other staff superbly and catered to my unpredictable schedule. I would regret it if I fired her for interrupting me at a very inopportune moment. I was a rational man, a successful businessman who didn't make rash decisions based on impulse or out of anger, so I composed myself before I formed a response.

"Oh my gosh, I'm so sorry," Cat said, vaulting out of the

hot tub, shivering into a towel over her dripping suit and heading for the French doors, "I'll get that. You don't have to put my stuff in the dryer."

"No, please, I would be happy to dry the clothes. I didn't know what you wanted to be done with them—" Clara broke off.

Cat stood before her, dripping and apologizing, completely adorable. Clara was obviously mystified, particularly by someone who didn't want to be waited on. I watched with a little amusement as my housekeeper argued with her about who would do the laundry. Within moments, Clara had produced more towels, was trying to help squeeze out Cat's streaming wet hair, and they disappeared into the house together. I got out of the hot tub and collected the champagne glasses and bottle with no small annoyance. That moment was gone.

I dried off and changed, then found Cat in dry clothes in the kitchen having hot tea with Clara. I cleared my throat.

"We'll talk later," Cat said to her with a smile. "Are you jealous?" she asked me.

I took her hand, liking the feel of her palm against mine, and led her into the living room. She sank onto the custom leather sofa and curled her legs beneath her.

"This is nice," she said, "do you know how much I like your hands?""Oh, really?" I said archly.

"Yeah. I mean, there's no point my being embarrassed. You already know I have a longstanding crush on you and even held on to your magazine cover for wicked purposes. So would it blow your mind to know that when we met and you shook my hand, I damn near moaned?" she said. I felt a rush of heat climb up my body at her words.

"I remember a certain something in that touch myself," I said.

"We're not talking a little spark or sizzle. This was serious chemistry. I thought you'd burn me down with one touch."

"I'm glad you liked it. I had no idea my handshake was quite so...potent," I teased. She laughed.

"Potent? You have no idea what an impression you made."

"And I hadn't even kissed you then."

"I wasn't just star-struck either. First of all, I got to go backstage and meet Justin Timberlake once when I was in high school. Not the same reaction at all, and I even had a picture taken with him. He put his arm around me and everything. Nope, no chemistry."

"I do believe that's the first time I've been compared to Justin Timberlake, favorably or otherwise," I said, "But he and I are rather different physical types. I prefer to think of myself as—"

"Not boy band material? Yeah, I can see that," she laughed.

"I was going to say more serious and less likely to bleach my hair and get a perm."

"Those were the glory days," she giggled, leaning over to kiss me, "And I'd take you over JT any day."

"I'll take that," I said, kissing her back.

"So have you been all these places?" she said, sinking lazily into my arms, indicating the framed black and white photos on the wall flanking the fireplace.

"Yes. On the left, that's St. Moritz. On the right, you see the skyline of Bangkok at night as well as a few shots off the coast of my island."

"Oh, your island," she said wryly. "Have you always taken pictures like that?"

"I've always shot photos, yes, but it took me several classes and a great deal of practice to reach the point where any of them were worth looking at."

"They're beautiful. I like that there's something personal in here, not just a lot of expensive things chosen to look good together. Not that it doesn't look good."

"It's funny that you said that. This is the first place I've lived where I didn't hire a designer. I chose things I loved and that meant something to me."

"So was this your great grandfather's couch?" she joked.

"No, but I chose the fabric and the style. Had it made to curve the way I wanted it. Because I envisioned myself sitting like this, watching the flames while it rained outside."

"It isn't raining."

"True, although I love the sound of rain, but in my mind, I didn't imagine having you here, rain or shine. I like this better."

"Wow," she said with an almost shy smile, "you are very charming. Has anyone told you that?"

"A few times, perhaps," I said with a smile, "I can say this is the best day I've had in a very long time."

"Me, too," she said. "Maybe the best one ever."

"Better than the hot tub with your friend's brother and the soggy tissues?" I challenged with a grin.

"Yeah, even better than that. And you know how sexy that had to be."

Eventually, I showed her around the house. She tried out the rowing machine in the gym, claiming she'd always wanted one, and she said the library was her definition of paradise. Apparently, she'd wanted a library of her own even more than she had wanted a rowing machine. Her enthusiasm was contagious. I stole kisses in every room, but I didn't try to push it farther. It felt too perfect, almost fragile. I wanted her but somehow didn't want to spoil the day either. So I contented myself to hold her hand, press her against the wall with hot kisses and glide my hands up her sides, down her arms, teasing her. I wanted her to go home and be unable to stop thinking about me. I wanted her as keyed up, as on edge as I was. Sometimes delaying gratification made it so much more satisfying.

I treated the entire day like foreplay. Sweet, playful, romantic, sensual. I knew seduction well enough to play the long game, to win her over, to tantalize her until my mouth, my hands, my body would be all she could think about. Then she would be mine.

Mine was a word I thought about far too often with Cat.

After I took her home, I wondered again if it was a mistake. If this was a woman who could match me in every way or only a very savvy young opportunist who was willing to give me enough rope to hang myself. Because she already had a case for harassment if she wanted one, enough to get a fat settlement or a book deal or both. She could take down my reputation, my company. I had to trust in her desire for me, her goodwill. Trust was not in my skill set. That skill set had served me well up until this point, but it pained me to doubt her, to wonder if she was far more a danger to me than I had imagined.

I would call her to my office. I would apologize to her if I had behaved in any way that offended her. I might have to forget the seduction, the foreplay, the payoff. I didn't want to forget it. It promised to be unforgettable.

I was a man who made intelligent, logical decisions. Not a man who played with fire. Not a man who was beginning to like the burn.

19

CAT

It was ten in the morning on a Monday. I had more energy, more excitement for work than anyone had ever had on a Monday in the history of the world. Because I had put on my black lacy underwear and bra, and I intended to use them. Conventions be damned. I wanted him. He wanted me. It had been all I could do not to howl in frustration the day before when he took me home and kissed me at the door and left. So when I got the call to go to his office, I hoped very strongly that it was a private appointment, that our meeting would be scheduled to last at least an hour and a half.

In his office, he stood behind the desk, looking morose.

"Are you okay?" I asked, advancing toward him. He put up a hand as if to stop me.

"I'm fine. I wanted to inquire how you were," he said stiffly.

"You wanted to inquire? What did you think I pulled a muscle getting out of the hot tub? I'm fine, but you're acting weird. What's going on?"

"It occurred to me that my initial stance on any relationship with you was likely correct. It is unseemly for a man in my position, wealthy and, in fact, head of the company for which you work, to become involved with a subordinate such as yourself. Please understand that there will be no repercussions for you. No lost promotions or unfair job reviews. You don't have to agree to see me outside of work in order to keep your job or advance your career."

"Are you done with your weird little speech? Because you must be in your head right now, making up problems. I'm here with you because I want to be here. You want that, too. There's no way you're a good enough actor to pretend that kind of passion that I felt yesterday with you. Regardless of the fact that you are gorgeous enough for Hollywood, I think you're just—scared. I don't know why, but it's stupid, so cut it out," I said.

I wasn't about to unpack everything crazy about his apology. I just wanted to skip to the part with the kissing. I rounded the desk and reached for him. This time, he looked almost anguished. Like he wanted to resist. Then he engulfed me in his arms, his mouth claiming mine until I was breathless, heart pounding in my ears. I could feel the force of my pulse throbbing through my body, a great, heated thrumming throughout my body.

"If that's how you feel," he said raggedly against my throat, "we should have lunch together and discuss what we want from each other in the way of a relationship."

"Good, let's go to the Royalton Arms."

"That's a hotel."

"Very good, I think you understand me," I said. He grinned, a predatory smile that made my toes curl. I was so glad I'd worn my black lace.

The time until noon passed slowly. I worked at my desk and tried to act normal. Then I reapplied makeup and put perfume in my cleavage before I left for lunch. I'd never been to a hotel midday, never had a secret rendezvous or a real lover to meet clandestinely. The anticipation made me shaky, thrilled but nervous. I asked at the front desk for Mr. Waltham's room and they sent me right up, giving me a key card and everything. I entered the suite, the curtains drawn to make it dim and secluded looking.

Brent was there, his jacket off, his sleeves rolled up. I went to him. He caught me in his arms, kissing me, unbuttoning my blouse as my hands flattened on his strong back. I just reveled in being kissed with that demanding heat, his relentless tongue doing dark, delicious things to me already. I stopped being passive once he got my blouse off. I dragged my hands through his hair and guided his head down to my chest where he kissed the swell of my breast above the lace of my bra. Then he pushed down the strap and slipped his hand inside the lace. It was an incredible turn on, his cool, rough fingers after the silky lace of the bra. My nipples hardened instantly. I clutched at his hair and hooked my leg around one of his just to have him closer.

This was a love affair. I thought wildly. This was what it felt like to take a lover—heady and confident and lucky as hell. I tugged at his tie until I got it loose. He pulled it over his head and shrugged off the shirt I'd unbuttoned for him. The first shock of his skin on mine, my bare stomach against his as he lifted me, my legs going around his waist—the sensation was white-hot. All my nerve endings seemed to fire at once, and I wound my arms around his neck. He carried me to bed, a four-poster bed that looked antique and beautiful. But I couldn't pay any attention to the décor with Brent Waltham between my thighs.

He laid me down on the bed with great care and climbed up beside me. He kissed my face, my neck, and my collarbone. I ran my hands up and down his bare, muscular back like I'd been dying to since before I ever met him. The hard glitter of his eyes seemed to tear through my defenses as he looked his full at me, dragging my skirt down and tossing it to the floor, hooking his fingers into my panties and taking them down, crushing them in his hand. Seeing that delicate dark lace crushed in his palm made me catch my breath with arousal. Then Brent took me by my thighs and pulled me to the edge of the bed. He lifted my legs so they rested on his shoulders, spreading me wide.

My breath sawed in and out, eyes fixed on him. With one long finger, he traced my cleft, fingertip pressing into my wet pussy, feeling how drenched I was for him. He made a satisfied sound and unzipped his pants. I felt a tremor go through me then, thrill and fear mixed in a heady cocktail. I felt the crown of his cock against my cleft, big and flaring, hot and slick. I arched off the bed. His big hand stilled me, fanning across my belly, pressing me down on the mattress. I craned my neck to see as he thrust into me with one mighty push. I bowed up with a cry, taking it as he held me down. My legs jerked, my body quivered. He stroked my thighs as he worked in and out of me, his fingers playing closer and closer to my clit as I held my breath with every thrust, bracing for the impact of that huge cock driving into me. I loved that I could take it, every inch of him. I loved my bare legs on his shoulders, the view I had as he lifted my hips so I could watch him fuck me.

Too soon, I was moaning every time his cock left me, my wet sex clinging to him, then crying with a high pitched whine as he thrust back in. I reached up and he caught my hand in his. Our fingers laced together, palm to palm. I came, the orgasm seeming to rip me in two as I wailed in the throes of it. Brent moved over me, onto the bed, never breaking our joining. He stroked my sweaty hair back from my forehead and kissed me, his thrusts growing faster, less measured, his kiss off-center and frantic. I clung to him, arms around his back as he arched and gave a shout and climaxed within me. He caught me in his arms and held me, rolling us so he lay on his back and pressed me to his side. He kissed my hair, my face, and drew the blanket over us. I trembled, felt weak but replete. I could say nothing, and neither could he. It had been shattering, a joining and breaking apart so that we were not the same afterward.

In his arms, I slept. We both slept, tangled up together. Then, slowly, we awakened and with the tenderest kissing and touching, we made our way to the shower. He washed my hair and kissed my neck, made me feel cherished, magical. Scrubbed clean and wrapped in a plush hotel robe, I combed out my hair and dried it. He came up behind me, rubbed my shoulders and bending, kissed my cheek. He was magnificent, the muscles of his chest and back, his strong legs, and his deft hands. I looked my fill. I had imagined this hundreds of times, but in my mind, it was a quick tryst, heated and almost detached, purely physical. This had gone well beyond the physical. This was chemistry and connection, his fingers lacing with mine and the deep resonance of our eyes meeting, of every touch.

I might have set out to have a torrid affair, but instead, he had been so tender, so sensuous, so passionate—everything to stir my heart as well as my body. After I was dressed, makeup reapplied, I met him in the sitting room. A cart of room service awaited me, the food beneath silver domes.

"I promised you lunch," he said.

"It's like 2:30," I protested.

"And we still need to eat," he said.

We sat and ate a delicious chicken Marsala with crisp chardonnay. He fed me a spoonful of berries with zabaglione, and I sighed.

"Orgasms and dessert, too? A girl could get used to this."

He kissed me, the sweet cream still on my lips. I melted into his arms. I never wanted to leave.

20

BRENT

At the office, I tried to forget. Vivid flashbacks of our tryst in the hotel bombarded me. Cat's hand sweetly reaching for mine at the moment of climax, the way she'd been trusting and open and passionate, so lovely. I had never wanted to let her go.

Work had to be completed, the day's obligations met, but when she messaged me, I didn't answer. I felt unsettled, almost panicked. As if something tremendous had occurred, something that could undo my entire life as I knew it. I felt undone, unspooled by the lovemaking. That was what it had been. It was no frantic, physical coupling to satisfy an attraction. I wasn't satisfied. I wanted more. Nothing about my ferocious desire for Cat had been slaked by those stolen hours in a hotel room. More than anything that infuriated me. She had some hold over me, something that kept me wanting more. Her opinions, her humor, her passion. I felt tethered to her, beholden to her. As if I could not do without her. It was an alien feeling that struck fear in my heart.

After her third message, I replied curtly that I was

working all evening. Then I proceeded to do just that, returning calls and messages, looking over reports and examining projections for the next quarter. Then, around eleven, I changed my mind and texted her, asked if I could go to her place.

Perhaps I had stumbled into her arms as the culmination of a perfect storm. The confluence of Tom's impending wedding and that damn holiday card from my ex-wife. I had experienced unusual pangs of envy, and my attraction to Cat became confused in my mind with a latent desire for a wife and family. And it was ridiculous, but far more possible than believing that I was falling for a twenty-four-year-old employee.

I never considered myself easily confused or someone who had difficulty seeing things clearly, but I was ready to attribute my distress to some confusion of the mind rather than accept the fact that I could be experiencing something damned inconvenient and embarrassing like a real infatuation with this girl. Thinking of her as This Girl helped actually. If I thought of her as Cat, who made me laugh and kissed like the devil incarnate, then it was impossible to dismiss her from my mind. If I labeled her This Girl and considered that she was too young and improper as she worked for me, then it was easier to separate myself from this preposterous idea of having feelings for such a creature.

Just as I had comfortably reassured myself that I was overworked and tired, that she had no hold over me whatsoever, she called me.

"So, you're all done and you can come over?" she said. Her voice sounded happy and excited. I rubbed my chest with my hand absently, trying to get my pounding heart to calm down.

"I'm finishing up at the office," I said gruffly.

"So you can come over? I mean, I don't have pictures of my private island or anything, but I promise to give you a welcome you'll remember," she said, her voice dropping almost to a purr. Dammit.

"I'll be right over," I said.

I cursed myself all the way there. My resolve and my better judgment had flown right out the window at the mere suggestion that she'd be there, happy to see me, ready to be back in my arms.

This attraction to her was impossible to resist. It was unsettling at best. At worst, it was something I'd have to find a way out of, some manner of self-preservation before my professional life lay in wreckage. I had come too far for too many years to waste it all. Cat's presence in my life was certainly temporary and unlikely to do anything but damage both of us in the long run. I had to talk to her about it, as much as I dreaded the display of emotion likely to come from it.

I couldn't allow my attraction to derail my intentions again. I would hold fast to my purpose, to let her down gently, but to declare firmly and clearly that we would not continue any personal involvement or intimacy. No matter how unparalleled and fantastic that intimacy had been. That didn't matter at all. Obviously.

21

CAT

As soon as he entered my apartment, I knew I'd have a fight on my hands. He was visibly tense, his posture stiff and hands at his sides. He had kissed my cheek diffidently as if I were an aunt of whom he was not terribly fond. It was a dutiful kiss, dry and passionless. I scowled at him.

"You have *got* to cut the crap."

"Have got is redundant," he said coolly.

"Oh, so this again? We had sex. Quit being such an old woman about it. It was amazing, and I'll never forget it. As a matter of fact, I wouldn't mind doing it again. Because this affair we're having? It is NOT going to consist of you pushing me away and acting weird and then us having make-up sex. So if you want to be with me, be with me. But don't whine about it and apologize. You like me. We have fun, we have incredible sex, and we want to keep doing that."

He frowned at me, "That is an oversimplification. You're discounting the age difference, the power dynamics.

The potential ramifications of an ongoing affair between a junior employee and the CEO."

"Say more of that. It's super sexy," I deadpanned with a roll of my eyes. "You are so dramatic I could die."

"Excuse me? I am not being dramatic. This is reality. You are an employee of Astley Corp—"

"Excuse *me*. I've seen my direct deposit notice; I know where I work. Fast forward to the part where you're paranoid that my existence will destroy your career because someone, someday might find out that you are a man who has sexual relations with women. Instead of an environmentally conscious eunuch with a good reputation for keeping out of obvious trouble."

"My sexuality is not the issue. The issue is the fact that you work for me, and you're too young and nothing good can come of this. Scandal and—"

"Despair and locusts? Yeah. Got it. No drama here," I scoffed. "Do you think being with me will also make the hard drives meltdown at work and send the stock market into a tailspin? You're blowing this out of proportion completely. It was just sex."

"No Cat. That was *not* just sex," he said, seeming offended.

At that point, I started to feel tingly and become aware that this was getting good. It was becoming the kind of erotically charged verbal sparring I'd fantasized about after I'd met him. But I was growing weary of his objections to the affair that we had already begun.

"So what was it?" I challenged, stepping closer to him, ready to go toe to toe. There was no way I was letting him paint me as a victim being exploited by her boss.

"It was—"

"What?" I pressed.

"Unexpected."

"What did you expect to happen? We checked into a hotel in the middle of the day, and I didn't plan on playing checkers," I said.

"Clearly I understood the objective was to consummate—"

"More of that dirty talk, please," I said, irritated.

"Everything was more intense, more intimate than I had expected."

"We agree on that," I said grudgingly. "But if you say objective and consummate again, I'm leaving."

"You live here."

"I know. That's how annoying you are when you're all stuffy like that. You act like sleeping with me was the end of the world."

"It felt like it might have been," he said. Something in me shifted, melted at those words. He had felt it, too. I looked up, met his eyes in the silent tension of the moment.

He snapped the thread of that tension by taking my face in his hands and kissing me. Brent kissed me, his tongue in my mouth like he'd never let me go. I got my hands on his skin, hot and smooth. My arms wrapped around his neck. I stroked his tongue with mine, questing and tasting, that urgent need to be together again, eclipsing every argument.

Not waiting to be carried this time, I led him to the bedroom. I was about to quip that it was hardly the Royalton Arms when he peeled off my nightgown, leaving me bare before him. He shucked his trousers after kicking off his shoes. Brent climbed into my bed with me, the sheets cool and crisp on our bare skin.

"I want to see you," he said huskily, drawing me on top of him.

Then everything went frantic and passionate, a bright fury of legs and mouths and fingers. Every restraint burned away as he guided my hips down over his powerful erection. The first thrust of that cock into my tender pussy made me wince a little, but we didn't slow down. There was nothing but the urge to be closer, to bring each other to a screaming completion. Even as he rocked into me, guiding me with a big hand on my hip, he drew me down and kissed me, stroked my heaving chest as a rivulet of sweat trickled between my breasts. His fingers plucked at my sensitized nipples. He plunged into me, stirring his cock inside my folds until I shuddered a hard, intense orgasm, shattering around him. Brent thrust up into me rapidly, deeply and came. I felt the hot rush of his orgasm and shivered from it, from the primal thrill it gave me. I sighed with satisfaction, collapsed on his chest. Our bodies fused together as he kissed me again.

Brent wrapped his arms around me, turned me so that he was spooned up behind me, and we slept. Sleeping in his arms was an exquisite pleasure all its own. One from which I might never recover at all. Sometime deep in the night we made love again, half asleep but reaching out for each other, needing that satisfaction of that touch, that joining. I woke in his arms, splayed across his chest with my hair a mess.

Never had I been happier than in that moment, propping my chin on my hands and looking into his handsome, sleeping face. When he stirred, it was only to pull me more securely and comfortably into his arms. We drifted back to sleep together, waking around eight after turning off alarms and kissing each other back to sleep repeatedly. He skipped his run. I messaged Kim that I needed a personal day and I'd fill out the online form for my personal leave request.

"That wasn't necessary," he said. "I could have written

you a boss's note. It's like a doctor's note, only a bit differently worded. Please excuse Caitlin Sherman from work today as she needs to spend the day in bed. Boss's orders."

I giggled and kissed him again. And again.

22

BRENT

Waking up in Cat's bed in her cozy apartment felt like it could become addictive. Her sleepy smile and her eager kisses were all I could ever want. I felt complacence sinking into my soul. My ambition eroded. Thoughts of a legacy, of scholarships and libraries established in my name faded from my mind. I didn't want to think of the noble future, but of the intoxicating present. The moment in which Cat had curled up in my arms, head cushioned on my shoulder and dropped off to sleep as though she trusted me more than anyone in this world. That had been humbling and made me feel strangely protective of her. As if she were suddenly rendered fragile or in any way in need of my protection.

This woman. The one who told me my protests were dramatic crap. Who wasn't intimidated or afraid to stand up to me or anyone else. She needed no armor, no insulation from the slings and arrows. Perhaps instead she might be my shield, helping to buffer the agony of navigating a real and deep feeling that was previously unknown to me.

I wanted to stay in her arms and in her bed forever.

Despite practical concerns and responsibilities. Despite duty and training and experience. I found that I surrendered so readily, eagerly even to the ease and pleasure.

We languished in bed for hours, even after she responsibly requested a personal day from her supervisor. She had been conscientious about that—not asking me to say we were working out of the office for the day or on a special project. I would have gladly made an excuse for her, for our absence, but it would have been conspicuous. People would take notice, speculate that we were together. I wasn't ready to deal with that scrutiny, with the potential for scandal.

Tom's wedding was a chance to take a step back, get my head on straight. I just had to convince myself to leave that bed, to climb out of her arms intentionally. When every impulse I had told me to stay, to pull her closer. I indulged myself. I won't make excuses for that. I held her in my arms, inhaled the vanilla scent of her shampoo and shut my eyes because it was what I wanted. It felt good. It was as simple and as complicated as that.

Eventually, she stirred and turned over, a lazy smile lighting her face, "Hey, you. I'm glad you're still here."

"You thought I'd leave?" I said, "Sneak out?"

"Maybe," she said.

"I never want to leave. Unfortunately, I have to because I'm going to my friend's wedding. I'll be out of the office and out of town for a week. May I call you while I'm gone?"

"Yeah, it's safe to say you can call me," she said, kissing my cheek.

I kissed her thoroughly and got up. Within minutes I was dressed and gone.

23

CAT

I napped for a while after he left, then showered. It had been the most magnificent day and night of my life. I felt resplendent, glowing. Happiness must have shimmered all around me. Wrapped in my favorite blue robe, I handled work emails, messaged Kim that I'd definitely be at work in the morning. Then I talked to Sarah Jo.

"You've really only slept with, what, one or two guys before? So saying it was the best sex of your life is like saying the second roller coaster at the park was the wildest one. It's one out of two," she said.

"Fine, it was the best sex of anyone's life. In history. Like if you researched it, there would be some Italian guy in like the nineteenth century, and then Brent."

"As in your boss."

"No, Kim's my boss. This is the CEO."

"So he's *her* boss. Which means he's so far up the food chain from you that it's–"

"Do not say Weinstein. This is nothing like that because of attraction and enthusiastic consent and nothing at all to do with jobs or promotions or getting fired or anything. It's just a workplace romance. With phenomenal Greek god sex."

"I thought you said Italian?" she said.

"Fine, maybe it was some Greek guy in history who has his name engraved on a plaque somewhere. But he should make room for Brent's name."

"That's kind of my concern here, Cat," Sarah Jo hesitated, "I'm not trying to pee on your parade, but are you sure that he's ready to have this attached to his name. And by this I mean romancing the intern?"

"I am not an intern. I'm an HR associate. May I remind you we are both of legal age?"

"Yeah, and he has been of legal age since before you were born," Sarah Jo said. "And don't bother telling me to butt out because I love you and want to protect you."

"Yes, please protect me from the handsome, wonderful man who gives me earth-shattering orgasms. Call the police," I wisecracked.

"Such a smart mouth," she said, "you know your mama would smack you for saying that word."

"Orgasms. Yeah. I'm not saying it to her. I'm saying it to you. I'd ask you not to tell, but you'd fall over in a dead faint before you could say that word to my mama," I laughed.

"No kidding. I want you to be happy And I want you to protect yourself and take care of yourself."

"I will. And I'm very happy. How's life back home?"

"It's about the same, thanks for asking. We all miss you a bunch."

"Miss you, too. Love you," I said and hung up.

I didn't mention the wedding he was going to. The one in the Greek Isles on his oldest friend's yacht, where his closest friends would be gathered for a celebration. I wished so much that he had invited me, and that he had wanted to share that with me and to introduce me to the people who were most important to him.

It would have been awkward for him, I told myself. Bringing a new employee many years his junior to an event with his nearest and dearest. He wasn't ready for that, and neither was I. Having sex didn't make the relationship more serious, more permanent—probably. It did to me. Everything felt vibrant and glorious and a little terrifying. So much so that I was bruised by the fact that he hadn't invited me to accompany him to the wedding.

The only conclusion I could draw was that he didn't want his friends and colleagues to know about me. I had been fine with sneaking around until it came time to do so. Then I wanted him to be as proud of me as I was of him. The fact that he wasn't, that he hesitated to take that step was unsettling. It hurt. It took some of the shine off my joy and made me question things.

I was overanalyzing, so I made myself stop. I called Heather and a few of us went out that night. My story was that I had a crown fall out and had to go to the dentist so I missed work. Everyone admired my teeth and Heather even asked if I had a whitening treatment while I was there because my smile was gorgeous. I hugged her.

On our second margarita, Heather asked if I was going to see her brother again. I pasted on a smile, "He was so great, but there just wasn't a spark. It was fun meeting him though, and I'm really flattered that you set me up with someone you love so much."

"Aww, you're so sweet," she said, "I have another brother though..."

"Um, that would be weird. 'Hi. I work with your sister, and I went out with your brother once, so now it's your turn,'" I said with a nervous giggle.

"You've got to get out there. We love spending time with you, but doing your laundry isn't exactly weekend plans," Kim said.

"I know. I just—I don't know. Maybe in the spring."

"My cousin Mike's divorce will be final around Valentine's Day," Kim offered. "He's a great guy. If you want to meet him, I'd be happy to set it up."

"Oh, thanks. I'll keep it in mind. I'm sure he's a terrific guy," I said, thinking, *What, two seconds after his divorce? No thank you!* And *Yeah, who would want sexy boss Brent when you could have recently divorced Mike?* I smiled and downed my margarita.

I fielded offers to fix me up with all kinds of relatives, exes and friends-of-friends before I managed to steer the conversation to something else. It was a fun evening, but on my way home I got a text from Brent that he was getting ready for takeoff.

"Hope you have a good pilot," I said.

"I'm the pilot," he replied.

Oh God. He flew planes too. He looked like that and flew planes, and I watched Top Gun way too many times growing up. Once I was home it was just me, my advance copy of Forbes, and sexy pilot fantasies.

2 4

BRENT

The deck was strung with twinkle lights. A string quartet played softly, and candles and white rose petals adorned the tables. The reception was stunning, tasteful and elegant. A gourmet buffet of the couple's favorite foods was on offer, and there was plenty of Moët to go around. It had been a lovely wedding. I'd caught up with old friends, held my godson River Brent through the ceremony and let him chew on my very expensive Hermes silk tie.

By eleven pm on the second night, at the wedding reception, I was completely done. If I'd had my helicopter, I would have made up an emergency and left. The whole event, surrounded by colleagues and friends who flashed pictures of their new homes and vacations and talked about their families—it felt like a shoe that didn't fit comfortably any longer.

I admitted it to myself at last. I wished Cat was with me. That I could show her Santorini and the Adriatic Sea. I knew perfectly well while I watched Tom kiss the bride that I had feelings for Cat. The kind of feelings that made a man of my age and station ridiculous. I had looked scornfully at Malcolm for years over his increasingly younger women, his youthful, pretty wives who clearly married him for money while he was besotted and idealistic about romance. The fact that he seemed happy did not make him appear less absurd to me. Marrying a woman so much younger, so much less accomplished simply made men like me look older and desperate and deluded.

So my feelings for Cat could be nothing more than the vanity of a man who knew his age and mortality, right? Or it could be love, the kind that songs were written about, but I couldn't risk it. I had spent my life above the fray, keeping my reputation upstanding. I valued my honor, my good name. So to appear as a middle-aged man who wanted to have sex with a twenty-four-year-old woman who only wanted his $30 billion, that would be catastrophic for me. It would damage the share value of my company and its public face. I was an entrepreneur and a philanthropist, and that was the legacy I had chosen. I did not want to be remembered as a very rich dirty old man that the thought sickened me.

This was foolishness I could not afford. It was a lapse in judgment that risked what I valued most, my character as a fair and honorable man who cared about stewardship of the planet for coming generations. Not the character of a man who cruised high school parking lots in his limo looking to pick up barely legal blondes. I would be a caricature. My board of directors would ask me to step down for the good of Astley Corp, and they would be right. My friends would ridicule me, my charitable patronages would rescind invitations. I would essentially stop being the man I thought myself to be and would become *ridiculous* and that was the word that stung me.

Instead of staying on for the next two days of revelry—the deep sea fishing and skeet shooting and wine tasting and shore excursions—I chartered a plane from the mainland and went to London. Astley had an office there, and I could look in on the operations. I settled into my flat and enjoyed the view of Hyde Park. It was such a beautiful city. I wished I could spend more time there. I had fish and chips in a pub I had been to many times before. I spent a few hours in the Tate Modern, even visited a work I had donated two years back, which was on display. I didn't want attention or a VIP tour, so I wore a ball cap and jeans and passed for any other American tourist. The anonymity was nice, peaceful. I was still lonely for Cat, but I would get over my foolish sentiments in time. It was a good thing the wedding had been timed as it was, so I could step away and think rationally before it was too late for the company and my reputation.

While I was in the London branch of Astley, I developed an idea. A potential solution that might work. It would not harm Cat's career. It would preserve my reputation. I tucked the possible answer in the back of my mind should things escalate. I was fairly confident that I was at the point where I could calmly and sanely express to Caitlin that, although I cared for her, it was an impossible situation. She could not fit into my life without the destruction of what I hold dear, and I would not want her to suffer the scandal, the remarks about gold diggers and trophy wives. It would end in resentment and regret. She was a clever woman who would understand the practical considerations.

If not, then there was always the office in London.

25

CAT

He called me once when he arrived in Greece. It had been a brief conversation. I had said I missed him. He said he would be back soon. After that, he had sent me one photo of the view from the yacht, which was so perfect it looked fake. Then, nothing. My good morning and good night texts went unanswered. I could blame international cell service or his being busy with obligations, but it felt like he was ghosting me. Like he was intentionally slipping away.

After what had been a shattering and perfect night together, after an intimacy I'd never imagined, he was trying to break it off with me. I would be sophisticated and cool about it. I would not call him crying. I would not shout recriminations. I would rise above. I would just stop messaging him. I would leave him alone and let him come to me if he wanted me.

I felt desolate and miserable. I even admit to crying in the shower the first morning I knew he'd be back at the office. Kim had to go to his office for something, so I knew he'd returned. I didn't even blink when she said that's where she was headed. I just wished her luck and went back to work. I would prove my mettle—productive and efficient and not letting my personal life affect my performance. That was the goal. No one wants to promote the girl who cries in the bathroom all the time about her horrible ex-boyfriend—even less so if the ex is everyone's boss. So I was thankful for the secrecy, the fact that everyone didn't know. I could pretend my dignity and my heart wasn't smashed to bits.

I finished my Christmas shopping online at lunch. I listened to people chat about what they were wearing to the staff holiday party on Friday night. I said I probably wasn't going. I didn't have a good excuse prepared though. So the next thing I knew, I'd agreed to go shopping with a few of the girls. I could not imagine wanting to buy a festive cocktail dress to wear in front of Brent, but slowly I convinced myself that it would be the best revenge, showing off what he let go of. It needed to be red, I decided because subtlety was so last year.

I met up with Kim and her husband before the party so I didn't have to go in alone. She hadn't indicated that she knew I'd been with Brent and that it was over, but she was a smart woman who missed very little. As observant as she was, it was difficult to believe she didn't know, but she was too discreet to mention it. Still, she was kind to me, and I didn't have to show up by myself. Heather came in right after us with her new boyfriend and the exciting news that her brother Andy aka Blandy was engaged! I felt like I needed to lie down—because here at the holidays I was dumped, but Blandy the boring date had a lifetime commitment going on. I swilled some champagne to toast his future happiness and dull my present misery.

We mostly stayed in our little HR group at a round

table eating the multitudes of good appetizers—the shrimp was fantastic—and drinking from the open bar and laughing too much. When the DJ started spinning Katy Perry and Ke$ha, the music of my high school years, I hit the floor with some of the HR girls. Kim and her husband danced and laughed. Heather and her boyfriend turned everything into a grind. We were having an amazing time.

I had seen Brent across the room at the beginning of the evening, and I'd spent a lot of energy ignoring him. Did I want him to see me in a hot red dress laughing and dancing and having fun without him? Absolutely, but I didn't count on him coming to speak to me or asking me to dance.

I said yes. Why did I say yes? I was supposed to be partying and getting over him, not proving that I was at his beck and call. My brain was yelling at me, but my heart had already accepted, and we were on the dance floor. It was crowded, a slow Bruno Mars tune from years ago that everybody seemed to know the words to. I let him hold my waist with my arms around his neck. We danced, started out as far apart as middle schoolers at our first dance. By the first chorus, I was nestled against his chest and his hand was in my hair. I wanted to cry because everything clicked in place and felt right. Nothing had felt right since the minute he'd left. I peered up at him without a word. I knew it was a pleading look. I knew I'd hate myself. I didn't care. I wanted him more than I cared about the consequences. Loving him made me reckless. And that's the only excuse I had.

He drew me from the crowd all the way to the elevator. He backed me up to the wall as soon as the doors slid closed, "I hear this is your second favorite one," he said huskily just before his mouth covered mine. I moaned when his tongue slipped into my mouth. My entire body rose to meet him, his hand sliding down to cup my ass while my fingers wove through his hair. On the dim, empty floor, he unlocked a board room.

We slipped inside, and in the silvery city light streaming between the window blinds, I saw that it was the same room where he'd scolded me for taking out my phone in a meeting. I felt a shiver of luscious anticipation when I realized that. I met his eyes.

"We had a meeting here," I said slyly.

"We're about to have a better one. I was going to resist and keep away. Until I saw you dancing in that dress and your laugh—God help me, I was undone. I had to get to you. I had to have you. If you don't want this, tell me now," he said.

Brent looked anguished, torn, in a way that wasn't very flattering to me, but I didn't care. I knew I could soothe him, remind him of what we shared together. That this was a language we spoke, a way I could reach him when he was too much inside his own head.

"I want this. I'm an idiot for wanting it," I said, "But I'm not ashamed. I choose this, no matter how it turns out."

Satisfied with my answer, Brent cupped my face in his hands and kissed me deeply, the strokes of his tongue stoking the fire in my body that already burned high. He kissed my bare shoulders as he unzipped my little red dress. It clung to my curves so that he had to push it down to the floor. He stopped for a moment, paused because he was stunned. I was naked beneath my new dress. It had built-in boning for chest support, and it curved close enough that I didn't want a visible panty line. So I had worn that dress and nothing else. I'd be lying if I said I hadn't hoped he would find that out first hand.

Everything was steamy and silent, the way he lifted me onto the table, the way he sat down in the chairman of the board's leather chair and took me by the hips, sliding me closer until my arms hooked over his shoulders. He feasted on me, my bare pussy quivering under the onslaught of his mouth. I came as he probed my lips with his fingers and lapped my clit with his wicked tongue. I rose up off the table as I came, my back arching. Suddenly, my body went off again unexpectedly because he pressed me down with a big hand on my belly, a hand whose thumb happened to start rubbing my clit furiously, mercilessly until I screamed and thrashed, weak from the relentless pleasure.

"You're soaking wet for me now," he murmured, standing up.

I levered myself up to a sitting position, my arms braced on his shoulders so I could watch. I wanted to see his cock pierce my body, watch him enter me and make that stretching fullness obliterate my mind again, releasing me into too-tender sensations and shocks of icy ecstasy. With one powerful thrust, he was buried inside my passage, my walls clamping down on him, trying to hold his immense size, trying to work up and down on him when I was so speared by his hard arousal that panting was the only thing that helped. I hung on to his shoulders. I'm sure I begged. I'm sure he gave me everything I asked for and more because there he was, holding my hips, pumping into me gently. I knew he was holding back, that it was exhausting him to restrain himself. I griped his face for a kiss, "Let go," I said, "You can let go now."

"Never, God, Cat, I'm never letting you go—" he groaned brokenly. Then he came, shaking and saying my name again and again.

"Let me take you home," he said into my hair as he held me. I sat on the edge of the table, leaning against him, resting in his arms as he stood, pants around his ankles, and stroked my back and hair.

"I don't know," I said.

"To my place," he said, "I have a penthouse near here. I want you to spend the night with me. Please," he said.

So I dressed uneasily and followed him. I knew people had seen us and knew how many security cameras there had to be. It both thrilled and disturbed me that he wasn't trying to keep us secret any longer. In his car, he told me that we would be there in five minutes. Then he told me to touch myself. Shocked, I met his eyes. In an instant, his wicked eyes gleamed. He took my hand, kissed it. Then he turned it over and licked my fingertips, sucking them into his mouth one at a time. Even that was incredibly sexy. Then he took my fingers, damp from his heated mouth, and pushed them down between my legs. He rubbed my wet fingers back and forth, guiding my hand with his as he used my wet fingers to stroke me. Mesmerized, I bit my lip to keep back a moan. When I could stand it no longer, the torment of his using my own hand on me, the tension in my body, the fear of the driver hearing us—I pushed his hand away and pulled him to me. We kissed, in a way too softly and sweetly—it was exquisite agony to have only the gentlest strokes of his tongue when I was trembling with need when I wanted more.

At the building, he unlocked a private elevator to the penthouse. As we rose to the top floor, he cupped my breasts through my tight little dress and fondled them, turning me on even more. My body responded to his touch, to every tug, every roll of his thumb across my pebbled nipple. The doors opened too soon, spilling us out, a tangled mess of limbs and mouths, straining to get closer. He pulled me into a bedroom, switched on a dim lamp. A broad platform bed, black silk sheets awaited us. My knees went weak at the sight. I looked at him. He kissed me, just locking our lips, letting them cling. I was his. If I hadn't been before, that kiss made me his as surely as a lock and key, as surely as a ring could have done. A ring I'd never have from him. I stuffed that voice down, the one that objected, and I let myself have this night, this man and those slick black sheets.

Brent stood while I removed his clothes, the suit jacket, the tie, the shirt. When I opened his trousers, I felt the thickness of his erection spring forth. I gripped it with my hand for a moment before stripping off the rest of his clothing. I wanted him naked. Wanted him vulnerable before me, as I stood in my red dress and stilettos, taking in the muscular, gorgeous body of the man before me. I would remember what he looked like all my life, the stacked muscles of his stomach, the valley of smooth skin at his hips, the strong thighs I wanted to ride. I licked my lips on purpose, to watch how it affected him, how his cock twitched in response. I sidled closer, kissed his cheek and whispered.

"Did you miss me?" I said.

"I missed you, Cat. Every minute on that boat—I left early and went to London, but I wanted to show you everything there. You'd love London. I couldn't enjoy it. I wanted to tuck you under my arm, hold you to my side as we walked, kiss you right in the middle of the street—" the words came streaming out of him like a confession.

"That could be dangerous in all that traffic," I teased, kissing just beside the corner of his mouth.

"Never. I would never let anything hurt you. You have to know that. Not even myself and my position. That's why this has to be—" he broke off.

Brent kissed me then as if he could no longer contain his

arousal. His iron control was slipping, and it thrilled me. I felt his hardness against my belly through my dress.

"I missed you," I said, "I even broke in my new copy of Forbes. I touched myself while I thought of you, Brent." The confession felt sweet, and his groan and his deep, almost punishing kiss felt even sweeter.

My back was on the silk sheets, and the weight of him was on top of me. He worked the top of my dress down to capture my nipples in his mouth one by one and wind me up with licking and sucking them. I stretched my arms out above my head decadently, letting him spoil me, but I locked my legs around him, making sure he knew I wasn't letting him stop. I palmed his head as he laved my nipple with his tongue, my other hand scratching his bare shoulder lightly, loving the light scrape of my nails on his skin and the way he reacted to it. He moved his mouth to my neck, sending shocks of pleasure down my body as he sucked the sensitive spot on my throat.

"Can't. Wait—" he ground out between gritted teeth.

With one big hand, he shoved my dress up and hitched my knee up higher to open me to him. He was in me then, hard and fast, pumping relentlessly, his big cock filling me till I was breathless and holding on, sucking his neck as he pressed me down into the bed and fucked me. He groaned, "Yesssss" once and bucked his hips as he emptied into me. The liquid rush of his orgasm made me clench, my inner muscles fluttering at the hot shock of it. A sharp, quick orgasm made me clamp down hard on his cock as I came around him, bucking under him. His mouth found mine. It had been quick and dirty, exactly the way I knew it would be when we reunited after he was gone. The coupling in the board room had only taken the edge off until we could get to a bed. Then we were together in the sheets, twisted up and kissing until we had to break apart breathless. Then he would pull me in again and kiss me some more as if he'd never get enough. My dress came off at some point during the night, my lips were swollen and bruised from his hard kisses, his shoulders scored by my nails deep in the night when he woke me with his mouth between my thighs. It was a dark blur of sex and sweat and pounding hearts.

In the early morning, when we were at last calm and sated, still holding hands palm to palm, laying side by side in those black sheets, I turned my face toward him.

"I love you, Brent," I said. It made me feel strong to say it like I had spoken the truth out loud instead of being afraid of it. I didn't wait expectantly with some innocent smile on my face. I knew he wouldn't say it back. His heart was so locked away, so compartmentalized that he might not even know love if he felt it. It had still mattered to me that I say it aloud and that I made sure to I own up to what I felt, to show him that it wasn't a weakness.

26

BRENT

I should never have brought her here. It was like I was an animal, and I'd lost all self-control. Everything that had felt so good, such relief in being with her and the staggering power of my release, had turned sour in one sentence. It was madness. Not even when I got married and divorced had I been this stupid and rash in my decisions.

She thought she loved me. That was it. The bucket of icy water in my face, the writing on the wall—whatever stupid metaphor would apply to the bed I'd made but wouldn't lie in.

"I'm so sorry," I heard myself say. *I sound like an asshole,* I thought, *We're in bed. She's naked. You don't break up with a woman in bed.*

"Don't be," she said, touching my chest lightly.

I sat up, sprang up is more like it. Away from her touch.

"I shouldn't have done this. I approached you at the party, I lured you away."

"You aren't the big bad wolf. You didn't lure me off my path," she teased.

"You were behaving in a far more mature fashion than I did. You didn't seek me out and drag me to an empty boardroom. You didn't insist on bringing me home afterward. You left me alone, completely civil and professional. I'm the one who couldn't stop. I should have done better and I will from now on because you're not for me, Caitlin."

"I get to decide that," she said. Her voice was so bold and sure, not shaken, not pleading like I expected. I was beginning to think she was stronger than me and had been all along.

"We can't be together. The age difference is ridiculous, and the discrepancy between my career achievement and yours. I'm a billionaire and the CEO. You were an intern from college last summer. We don't go together. It's ridiculous. The whole world will see that and make fools of us both. They'll call you a gold digger and worse, and I'll be the buffoon, the idiot who gave away half his fortune in a prenup for a piece of ass."

"I am not a piece of ass. And I'm worth more than half your fortune," she said, sitting up brazenly. "If you're not man enough to cope with some gossip, you don't belong on the cover of a magazine and you sure as hell don't belong in my bed. You have every right not to be with me, but your reasons are the only ridiculous thing about you."

"This is wrong. I'm so much older than you. You work for me. It's a serious mistake, and it's unacceptable. A man of character would never have done this, would never have gotten mixed up with an employee much less one so young."

"You're making this about an idea of an old, rich guy and a young, helpless girl. This is US, dammit, Brent!" she said forcefully. "It's NEVER been about age or money. Remember the lunch we had, and when you took my hand? Tell me that wasn't an honest moment of connection. Tell me you didn't feel more than creepy old man lust for me!"

"Thank you for making it sound as disgusting and base as it is," I said with distaste, "I blame myself profoundly for what I have done. How I have taken advantage of you, your youth and inexperience. I have abused my position, and I've behaved abominably. I don't blame you for hating me. I loathe myself at the moment. But I have an opportunity to prove that I'm better than what I have done. I can put an end to this with dignity and discretion, apologize to you, and conclude this shameful episode."

"You're making up a story where you're the villain, and I'm the victim. I am nobody's victim, Brent Waltham. You're too scared to admit that we're equals and I love you and you may even love me back. So you're pushing me away and taking back your ice-cold comfort zone. I'll be out of the way and things will be back to the way you like them. You're everyone's hero, and I'm back in my convenient little box in your mind labeled Secret Shame."

She had wrestled her dress back on and was yanking her hair back in a ponytail, "Dammit. I don't have a hair tie," she said absently. She let her hair drop messy and loose over her shoulders. She looked so sad and defeated and terribly young. I wanted to take her in my arms, which was exactly what started the whole disaster to begin with. I shook my head.

"You should go."

"I will."

She walked out. I heard the elevator. I raked a hand through my hair, pulled up the security camera on my phone and watched her leave the building. She didn't cry or hang her head or look upset. She walked out with shoulders squared, chin up, too strong to let me see her heartbreak. At the door to the building, she paused and looked up into the corner where the camera was. She held up one finger at the lens, flipping me off, and walked out of the door and out of my life. I laughed at her rebellious gesture, but the sound choked in my throat and didn't sound like a laugh at all.

27

CAT

A flurry of parties and dinners kept me busy until after the New Year. I mastered the art of looking delighted and a little distracted instead of sorrowful. After the first of the year, Kim assigned me to the team rewriting the interoffice relationships guide. We spent a lot of time together, our little team of four, researching and debating wording and constructing examples. We created two characters: Chad and Riley, for examples. We made up scenarios and explained the correct and inappropriate behaviors that could take place in the workplace in each circumstance. After a while, I felt like I was writing Chad and Riley fanfiction. Marc, one of my teammates, and I started a Chad and Riley ship where we texted back and forth ideas for their dates. His ideas were: "feminist film festival, popcorn with vegan butter, no touching," and "Irish step dancing class." Mine were "meditation class to help focus on not thinking impure thoughts at work," and "paint party to make team building encouragement door signs for their separate offices." Heather got in on it, and we had a blast. Then Heather and her boyfriend broke up, and the Chad and

Riley ship turned into the Marc and Heather ship. I felt left out, but I was happy for Heather. They kept inviting me out with them, so finally I agreed. We went out after work and had a fun time, ate some nachos. My beer tasted bad, and although Marc thought it was fine, I replaced it with a margarita. When the first swallow of a margarita made me run to the bathroom to puke, Heather was hot on my heels.

"You look terrible. I'm gonna take you home. You've got that virus that Kim's kid had last week. The fever and puking and aching. Here, come on," she got me a cup of water to rinse my mouth and put me in a cab.

I swear I slept for two days, only getting up to nibble a cracker, drink some Sprite and go pee. I had never peed so much in my life. I told Sarah Jo when she texted that I had the flu from hell—that it was puking, exhaustion, and too much peeing. On Monday, I dragged myself to work. I was still a little queasy, but I didn't feel as awful. It was probably just depression from being dumped by the man I loved.

Refocusing on my work and chewing peppermint gum all the time helped, but I still felt foggy and tired and wanted to hide in my bed all day. But I went to work, came home, ate and slept. I was in bed by seven every night, but it was still murder getting up twelve hours later. I was so miserable after throwing up my supper of toast and hot tea that I actually caved and texted Brent. In a queasy haze, I had messaged that I missed him. I wished there was a way to un-send that message. Especially since he never replied.

The fact that he didn't answer was appalling to me. He didn't ask how I was or say he missed me or wished me well. I was over for him. There was no point engaging with me on any personal level, even as friends probably. I was even more miserable and checked my phone way too much just in case he decided to reply belatedly. He never did.

We completed the handbook and got the news that it was approved by the board and uploaded it on the company site. Hopefully, Chad and Riley would help many future employees navigate the shark-infested waters of interoffice romance far more successfully than I had. I who had embarrassed myself by asking Millie how Brent was doing and getting a pitying look, but no answer.

I knew that Heather and Marc were still going strong, planning a weekend away together. It made me feel hopeless, like I was older, wiser, beyond such idealistic dreams as a weekend holiday together. We had never had that, Brent and I. Just a couple of stolen nights and a lot of drama and heartache. It had been worth it, though. To experience the kind of connection, the kind of love and intimacy I'd felt when we talked or snuggled or sat in a hot tub joking around and kissing. It had been real, no matter what Brent wanted to believe about it after the fact.

28

BRENT

It's difficult to throw yourself into your work when the woman you're trying to forget works ten floors below you. The idea of having her beneath me, even structurally, was uncomfortable. And I remembered how she felt underneath me in bed, every curve and hollow of her body, every scrape of her nails and every moan I swallowed from her perfect mouth. It was hell. It seemed very much like I had set my GPS for hell and ended up there. Surrounded by oblivious, productive, happy people who didn't sit in their offices trying to concentrate on work but thinking instead about the clever, feisty woman who worked ten floors down, who was laughing her laugh for some other man now.

Weeks had gone by, and somehow I managed to get by without seeing her. A month had passed since we were last in the same room together. Still, every elevator, every crowd in the lobby, got a close scan from my eyes in search of her beautiful face. The face I needed to stop thinking about. The eyes and smart mouth and throaty laugh and strong thighs I had to stop masturbating about because even if I had successfully banished her from my thoughts, my cock, my entire body cried out for her. I went to Club Nine Three and had a steak with Malcolm. His wife wanted another baby, and so did he. He told me that he felt almost ashamed of being so happy, of building this family in his fifties. It was a luxury, he told me, to grow old, and a greater one to be able to afford to do so in comfort.

"I've got things I never knew I wanted," he told me, "I already had everything I'd worked for—the boats, the planes, the homes. My only regret was letting you outbid me on that island off Belize. Then I got married again, and I didn't give a damn about Belize or anything else. Because I had it all. Then we had River. It keeps expanding. It's better than I deserve, better than any man deserves, Brent," he said, gnawing his cigar thoughtfully.

I sipped my bourbon and didn't respond. He was content. I was happy for him, but much like the zip file Tom sent me of his honeymoon photos, it was something I didn't care to explore. I turned the conversation to a startup I wanted to acquire, an adventure tourism company out of Idaho that sounded promising.

"Don't forget the one I bought up in Uruguay that time. The couple was using the zip line funding to buy drugs," he warned.

"Really? That was one mistake. You can't let one bad experience knock you out of the game because you don't trust anyone," I said.

He chuckled. Damn him.

"So, you and the intern at the Christmas party..." he said.

"She's not an intern," I said hastily.

"Mmm-hmm. That's relevant," he said, "Did you have a good evening? Was it just a one-time thing or is there more?"

"Go home and give your wife a hormone shot," I said sourly.

"Go home and grow a set. You always had brass balls when it came to business, but you're moping around over some girl because you don't want to commit?"

"That isn't an issue."

"Really? Then what is? Was something wrong with her?"

"No. Nothing. She was perfect. Funny as hell, gorgeous, smart, a total disaster," I said miserably, draining my drink.

"This perfect girl, did she only want what she could get —a payoff or a promotion?"

"No. She said—she loves me," I groaned.

"Congratulations. You're the luckiest bastard since me. A woman you don't deserve has made the massive error of falling for you. Now it's your job to make sure she doesn't regret it," he grinned.

"I broke it off. It was the worst mistake of my life getting involved with her. I've never, not even in my younger days, slept with an employee."

"Well, are you waiting for a gold star for that? Because you don't get one. The way I see it is, you can apologize to her and be happy, or you can keep it up with the sackcloth and ashes until she moves on and you have to send a gift to her wedding," Malcolm said.

"Are you trying to make me feel worse?"

"If that's what works, then, yes, I am."

"I don't need this," I said, getting up.

"This is exactly what you need. You wouldn't be acting like such an asshole if you didn't have a thorn in your paw. Tell her you want her back," Malcolm said.

"I'm leaving," I said, and left.

The next morning, she was in the elevator. The goddamn elevator of all places. I stepped in. We were not alone. There were three other people there. I glanced at her. My body reacted to the sizzle still there between us. Her eyes met mine, big eyes above her pale and hollow cheeks. She looked thinner, tired. It wrenched me to think I'd done that to her by breaking her heart, but it also decided on something I'd been avoiding.

29

CAT

I followed him out of the elevator. I touched his sleeve, the fine wool slipping out of my fingertips even as I tugged it. He turned around, as handsome as ever, and the bottom dropped out of my stomach.

"How have you been?" I asked coolly. I would not whine or plead.

"Busy, and yourself?" he said, his tone clipped, his manner hurried.

I nodded and turned to press the elevator button. I tucked my hair behind my ear and waited.

"Caitlin," he said, clearing his throat, "I've been thinking about you. If you have a moment, I'd like to speak with you."

My heart leapt. He had reconsidered, had realized how perfect we were together. Not just the phenomenal sex, but the energy between us, the zing of our banter and the shared sense of humor and the playful, loving way we had. *Please ask me over to do my laundry,* I thought, as a smile went ahead and bloomed on my face. I felt better than I had in weeks.

He indicated a pair of chairs flanking a floor lamp across from the elevators. He wasn't even wasting time taking me to his office. We wouldn't have privacy, which annoyed me, but his excitement and eagerness made me happy at the same time. I waited for him to reach for my hand. His hand on mine had been so much what I desired the last few weeks. The jolt of awareness, the sensual rush of his touch and the flawless way our hands fit together like puzzle pieces. That had been missing from my life in recent times.

"I've been thinking," he said again.

"Yes?" I prompted encouragingly.

"A fresh start would be best for both of us. This situation, the way it has been is full of tension. When you were in the elevator, I nearly took the stairs instead. And that is a great many stairs. You see how it is, working in the same building and living in the same city is problematic. I have commended Kim on the job your team did with the handbook. I'll be forwarding that commendation along with your credentials to the head of HR in our London office. I think it would be best if you relocated. You won't suffer any loss of pay or status, and you'll be given a stipend for relocation to help you with a deposit on an apartment and shipping your belongings. Everything will be in order for your arrival. If you're willing to go. I won't transfer you without your consent."

He said consent, reminding me of our long lunch, our innuendos and the excitement of that early attraction. I shook my head a little sadly.

If I couldn't be with him, it didn't matter much to me where I lived. I was good at HR and liked my team, but I wasn't so attached that I couldn't start over. Brent was sending me away. This reality resonated in my mind. He didn't want me back. He wanted me out of his sight permanently. He had said he was thinking of me when what he was really thinking of was how to be rid of me.

"I'd like to tell Kim myself. She's been very good to me," I said.

"I think it best if you make it seem that you requested the change. It connects you less with me personally."

"We wouldn't want that," I said hotly. "You being associated with a new hire, with some girl who had to be gotten out of the way."

"This isn't like that," he persisted.

"This is exactly that," I said, remembering my pride.

I wasn't going to ask to be allowed to stay. I wasn't going to make a fuss. It was somehow important to me that I didn't communicate to him how desperately I loved him. He had to know that I had offered myself to him with my eager smile, my wrong impression of why he wished to speak with me. And he had to realize, I knew he was rejecting me again. For the last time. I could not have forgiven myself for begging. It would have been too much humiliation after everything else.

So I was London-bound. I told my friends and my boss. I called my friends back home. And I got some boxes from the copy room to pack my stuff in. The company was buying out my lease, and I was getting seven grand for moving expenses. Relocating me out of his sight was not cheap, I guessed.

Within a week, I was on my way to my new home across the Atlantic. I had always said I wanted to travel. I just hadn't planned to spend my first airplane ride barfing in the convenience bag. I had envisioned some exotic destination, some romantic holiday. Not puking in a paper bag because my ex was sending me away. Sometimes things are not as glamorous as we imagine them to be. I was learning that the hard way. My first minutes on English soil were spent dry heaving in an airport trashcan. My new life was not off to an elegant start.

BRENT

My plan was a success. Cat Sherman was safely stowed in Astley Corp's London office, well on her way to a career promotion and out of my life. I waited expectantly for relief to set in.

I would feel better any day now, knowing with full confidence that I'd never lay eyes on her beautiful face again. My building was empty of any sign of her. I could relax, not concerned that I'd run into her in an elevator or hallway, not concerned about catching a glimpse of her in a crowd.

I would sleep well at night again, and I'd concentrate during the day. I'd get back into my routine of fourteen and sixteen-hour days and workouts and work dinners and charitable giving. There was nothing to remind me of Cat at all. Except for the sound of laundry in my own home, the sight of my hot tub or champagne glasses or my favorite restaurant for lunch which I never went to now. The boardroom I mysteriously stopped using for our monthly meetings because I said the glare was bothersome this time of year. The fact that I remembered every minute detail of Cat—the lilt of her voice, the quirk of her eyebrow when she was being sarcastic, the way she had loved the pictures I took myself and hung on my wall, and the way she fit against me in bed, on a couch, in a hot tub, against a shower wall. The way her mouth felt against mine when our tongues mated and I thought I could die like that and never be sorry, our lips locked together, tongues questing, our bodies straining to become one. The pale skin against black sheets, the play of her fingers on my chest idly drawing circles there with her fingertip as she fell asleep. Those peaceful, silent moments and the scent of vanilla from her hair—it was driving me mad.

I couldn't even meet Malcolm for dinner. He knew too much and enjoyed tormenting me with advice that I could never take. It was ridiculous. I was ridiculous. Even without her she had made a joke of me. And I didn't hate her. I lusted after her, body and mind. Nothing would satisfy me but to have her beneath me in my bed, her soft thighs dropped open to cradle my hips like we were born for it.

And the director's daughter, the one I'd taken to the opera, Ella—she was moving to the city and kept messaging me. She bothered Millie about my schedule and when I'd be free. Ella was apparently ready to be a wife again, and a corporate wife at that. She continually tried to tempt me with tickets Harold secured to more opera and ballet performances. I had Millie tell her I was busy. She refused to say 'busy for the next decade' despite my urging.

I didn't want to see Ella, suitable and undemanding as she might be. I didn't want to hear Tom gloating—it seemed to me like gloating—over his new marriage and Malcolm gloating about how they were going to do another round of IVF next month. I increasingly avoided everyone outside of work apart from my trainer. Circuit training was as horrible as I felt, so it was a good fit. I thought exhausting myself physically would help me sleep at night. But it didn't. Nothing did.

After two weeks, I rang Hubie, the COO at the London office to see how she was settling in.

"The girl you sent us? Well, she's quite competent when she's here."

"What does that mean? Is she on vacation already?"

"I don't believe so, but she's missed several days due to a stomach illness according to her supervisor. The first week she thought it was jet lag and missed two days, and this week it's been three. She's been round to the chemist's apparently to no result. If she were a new hire rather than a transfer with your special recommendation, I would have given her a formal warning for truancy by now."

"I understand. I'll see if I can discover what the issue is through Kim, her boss in HR on this end. They were quite good friends, so I expect Kim might have some insight. She wasn't notably absent in her five months here, only one personal day according to the file," I said. I remembered that personal day vividly, lying in bed all day with her. I cleared my throat, which felt tight at the recollection.

I'd look into things all right. I'd contact Kim and if she had no information, I'd call Cat myself and demand to know what was going on. I'd set her up with a perfectly good job and she'd turned truant there. I reminded myself that I'd banished her far from her friends and family to get her out of my sight because I was, in fact, a weak bastard who couldn't keep my dick in my pants where she was concerned, or my heart off my goddamned sleeve. The idea that she might be ill so far from home made my heart turn over.

CAT

Telling Sarah Jo made it real. I'd known for four days before I said it aloud.

"I'm pregnant. I've already got an appointment with a gynecologist here, and I'm keeping the baby," I said.

"Well, good afternoon to you, too," Sarah Jo said wryly. "Are you okay? What can I do?"

"You can tell me that I can do this, and everything is going to be fine," I said.

"Of course, it is. You're strong, and you have a lot of people who love you and will want to help out. I'll babysit. I'm fantastic with kids. I'll teach him how to plant shrubs."

"That's what I need, a baby trying to eat plants. Thanks."

"Are you going to stay in London?" she asked.

"I don't think so. It's a good job, but I can't risk word getting back to Brent that I'm pregnant. Timing-wise, he'd know it was his baby. I've spent most of the day looking for jobs close to home. I saved most of my relocation bonus, so that will help with moving back, I guess."

"Why don't you want him to know?" Sarah Jo asked.

"Because. He's a coward who would rather banish me to the other side of the damn Atlantic than admit he has feelings for me. Not to mention, he never asked for this."

"Um, excuse me," she said. "But you didn't get knocked up on your own. He was in the room, and I doubt you put drugs in his drink to have your way with him. So this is his responsibility. Why should you change your life and give up your job just to protect him from being upset? He sounds like a complete jackass and way too delicate."

"That's sweet of you to be protective, but he isn't like that at all. He's concerned with his reputation and this company he's built. It would make him look bad if I was known to be pregnant with his child."

"Then he SHOULD look bad, sweetheart. If it bothers him for people to know he slept with you, had feelings for you, broke your heart, and shipped you overseas for his convenience, may he shouldn't be such a douchebag if he is so protective of his good name!" Sarah Jo sounded ready to annihilate him.

"I love you, too, but he's the man I love, flaws and all, and I know it was a mistake for him to send me here, but it was a mistake for me to agree to it as well. I have a baby to think of and can't waste energy on being mad at him."

"Fine. I have plenty of energy. I'm going to get on Wikipedia and find out how to make a voodoo doll. Do you happen to have any of his hair or nail clippings?"

"Ew! No!" I laughed, "I'm gonna go look for a job. I miss you."

"Miss you, too. I can't wait to feed you chicken and dumplings and make that baby all chubby."

"I think I'll have to wait a few months before food sounds good again. Please don't mention meat or... anything," I said. "Bye."

"One more thing, sweetie. I don't think you have to leave the company. He's too busy being a billionaire to monitor your insurance claims. He's not going to check up on you. He doesn't sound like the kind to be concerned. You could probably try transferring back to the home office and get away with it. Say you're homesick, or you just broke up with your British lover and want to go home."

"I've been here for two weeks."

"But it would kill two birds with one stone. You fell in love at first sight, spent all your time with him, he got you pregnant. You fled home heartbroken."

"I got pregnant and found out within fourteen days?"

"You really know your body. You had a sixth sense."

"Pregnancy is not like that unless nausea is my new superpower."

"Puker Girl? It's like Super Girl but with bodily fluids."

I laughed, "You. Are the worst. Bye."

Still, there was no way I could stay with Astley. He'd find out and either be embarrassed and blame me or try to take my child. Because on paper, here was a childless fortysomething billionaire who might like an heir. My baby was not being raised by a nanny and sent to boarding school at age four. Hell no. If that meant doing this alone, then I was determined to make that work. I would make this okay. I was intelligent and strong, and I could be a single mother with a career. Plenty of women did it.

BRENT

Kim hadn't heard from Cat. Neither had anyone else in HR. So I demanded that Kim give me her updated contact information. I had already tried her old number, but it was disconnected.

I was at Club Nine Three with Drew and Tom when I got the message from HR that she had only updated her address. There was no new phone on file. She was unreachable, possibly ill, and alone in London. And it was my fault.

Drew was telling a story about the bracelet he was bidding on that once belonged to Princess Margaret when I held up my hand to interrupt.

"Sorry," I said, "I have to go."

"Is everything okay?" Tom said.

"I'm not sure," I admitted. As I walked out, I called to have my plane readied and file a flight plan.

I had considered calling her family, her emergency contact back in her small town, but I didn't want to alarm them. And I didn't want to explain why the CEO at her former office needed so desperately to contact her. *I think she needs me* was too complicated an answer to unpack with strangers. But I felt it down in my veins. That my woman needed me. That Cat was, for better or possibly worse, my woman. And if she needed me, there was only one place I wanted to be. By her side. In her arms. In her bed.

If she needed to swear at me and throw things and make me swear on a Bible I'd never push her away again, I'd do it. I deserved far worse. The only thing I couldn't tolerate was if she didn't want me back. I wouldn't allow myself to imagine defeat. Think only of victory—that had been the maxim that served me throughout my career, and it couldn't fail me now. I would picture myself kissing her, holding her, making everything okay again. A walk through the rain-slick streets of London at dusk, with Cat under my arm. That was the prize I was fighting for.

Fourteen hours later, tired and anxious, I arrived in London and got a taxi to her road. All along the street in shop windows I saw flowers. I saw placards with advertisements for Valentine's Day deals. Looking at my phone I realized that it was tomorrow—Valentine's Day was fast approaching. I bought every rose I could find, from street vendors and a chemist's shop that was open early. I couldn't stand being apart from her. I was worried for her well-being, but more than that, I had wanted only an excuse to cross an ocean and find her.

With an armful of roses in different colors, I reached her address. It was a nice building, and I likely disturbed a great many people with my ill-bred pounding on her door.

CAT

Half awake and disheveled, I went to my door to see who was pounding on it. I picked up my can of pepper spray in case it was someone hostile and not just a neighbor. Opening the door, I stared in disbelief.

Brent Waltham with a day's growth of beard and an armful of red and pink flowers stood at my door. Gaping, I stepped back to admit him. He dropped all of the tissue paper wrapped flowers on my table and advanced on me.

"What are you doing here?" I said, pushing my tangled hair back from my face.

Brent took my face in his hands and kissed me. Pouring all the emotion I'd thought he wasn't capable of into a single kiss, the tip of his tongue tracing my lips until I opened them and took his tongue in my mouth like the last breath of air I'd ever have. A sob escaped me. I gripped his wrists, never wanting him to let go or stop kissing me. Then he crushed me in his arms and kissed my hair.

"I love you. I'm a stupid bastard, but I love you. I'll do anything to have you back, to have another chance. You have to marry me, Cat," he said.

"No," I pushed back and he released me. I shook my head adamantly.

"No?" he said, crestfallen.

"No. I can't marry you. I—I'm pregnant. So I can't do that," I said, a catch in my voice. I braced myself for his anger, his fury. His rejection now that he knew I was pregnant, possibly on purpose to steal his money and reputation.

I took a step back, astonished as Brent Waltham, a two-time cover model for Forbes and renowned billionaire, dropped to his knees in front of me and caressed the curve of my belly.

"Are you really?" he said with wonder, cradling my hips in his hands.

I nodded, feeling choked up, afraid to believe he was glad. He kissed my stomach and wrapped his arms around me, laying his cheek against the barely-there swell of my stomach. I stroked his hair fondly, hoping the moment didn't break, hoping this fragile joy continued.

Brent surged to his feet and took me in his arms, kissing and kissing me, "My love," he said, and I could have sworn I felt tears on his face when I touched his cheek. Or perhaps they were my tears. It didn't matter.

Everything swelled into beautiful light and happiness. He wanted me. Wanted our baby. I didn't have to keep it a secret. I could share this with him, with the only man I had ever loved. I held on to him for dear life, kissing him back with all the passion I'd tried to hold inside.

He had come back for me, wanted me, before he knew about the baby. I cherished that, and took his tongue deeper in my mouth, giving as good as I took. His hands on my back moved lower, squeezing, rubbing sensuously until I drew back.

"You're new in town. Would you like to see my bedroom, Mr. Waltham?" I said.

"If you don't have an elevator, I guess a bedroom will have to do. Until I can get you home where you belong. God, I'm so sorry, Cat. I'd give anything to take it back. You're right. I was a coward."

"It doesn't matter," I said with all my heart, "you're here now."

"And I'm never leaving. Not without you."

It thrilled me to hear him say it. I showed him the way to my little bedroom with the sloping ceiling and dormer window looking out on a pretty street behind the building. I tried to point out the view, but he stood behind me and cupped my breasts, stroked my stomach and let me feel what his intentions were. I turned in his arms and tipped my face up to be kissed.

Brent kissed me so tenderly, with so much love that I thought my heart would burst from the joy of it. He lowered me onto the bed and stripped off my nightgown. He traced my sensitive, swollen breasts, licking and sucking them, and explored the soft curve of my belly, my full hips, my thighs. I was throbbing and wet for him, so responsive as if there was a surge of arousal in my blood from seeing the father of my child, as if my body responded to him even more lavishly because of the life growing inside me.

At once, he was stroking between my legs. It felt so good that I gritted my teeth to fight against it, wanting more, wanting it to last longer. In what seemed like only seconds, I was clenching around his fingers and writhing, riding his hand to a hard orgasm. Left shaking I clung to him, face to face. He stroked my cheek and kissed me again and again. Then he shucked off his clothing and rolled me beneath him, "Next time you can be on top, I promise," he said, "but

I've had nothing but thoughts of you beneath me since Christmas. I need this. I need you."

I had never heard sweeter words, and his kisses, his love-making gave proof of his passion. He petted and stroked me, stoking my arousal deftly and patiently. I could have taken all of him at once, but he indulged me, teased me until I was biting my lips to keep from begging him for it. With a sly smile, Brent finally, at last slid home with one beautiful thrust of his cock inside me. I watched his face transform with acceptance and awe and complete love. As he started to move within me, I felt another orgasm flare to life. I rolled my hips up to meet his thrusts, and before it seemed possible, we both spiraled into a blinding climax together, crying out and kissing and clinging to each other for dear life.

EPILOGUE

CAT - ONE YEAR LATER

We hadn't been back to London since our wedding on Valentine's Day of last year. Brent had no trouble getting a special license that day, and I had plenty of roses for a bouquet. It was a beautiful memory, but this one would top them all.

We had returned for our daughter's christening. Isabel Valentine Waltham, four months old with blue eyes and her daddy's smile. She gave a noisy cry in the church when they had the audacity to dribble water on her sleeping forehead. We had laughed, and I had stood with my husband's arm around me, so perfectly happy. Our precious child, making her first trip abroad and shouting in church. It seemed like a herald of things to come. She had a big personality already and seemed likely to wrap all the world around her finger with her charm just like Brent. He doted on her. No father could have been more enraptured with his infant. Although Malcolm teased that she should have been called Isabel Malcolm Waltham to return the favor from my husband's godchild being named in his honor. Already they joked about River and Issy getting married someday.

After we posed for portraits on the day, I let Alma, Issy's nanny take her back to the flat. It was, after all, our anniversary. Brent and I had plans to explore London together. We wanted to celebrate everything we had—everything we nearly lost because of pride so we got in the car and rode to our first stop. The London Eye. I had been too queasy to ride it the year before, so we had plans to kiss at the top of the city before going out for a romantic private dinner at sunset.

My husband—I never grew tired of calling Brent that—led me to a glass pod and I slipped in beside him on the bench. He wrapped his arms around me and kissed me as we ascended slowly.

"I know how much you like elevators, so I thought this would please you," he teased.

"You please me," I said, "Every night."

"I'm glad, but I was wondering what you thought of a trip, just the two of us. Maybe when Issy is six months old?"

"I'd love it, but I'm not sure I can stand to leave her," I said.

"What if we started with just a weekend away? And then stayed away longer when you feel ready. I want to get you alone, you see."

"Oh, what for?"

"For a son, I think. Or another daughter," he said slyly.

"Oh, you want more babies now? The man who never wanted a family?" I said.

"I never knew what was good for me until you came along and made everything else seem pointless. This is what I've needed all my life. You in my arms. Issy. And baby makes four. Or five. I wouldn't mind twins."

"Twins is it?" I laughed, "are you sure you have it in you? That might take a lot of practice. You'll need stamina."

"I work with a trainer. And don't forget, I've been on Forbes' cover twice. I hear I'm notoriously sexy."

"Potent even," I giggled.

"I'll show you potent. After dinner we have a suite at the Savoy, Mrs. Waltham."

"A suite all to ourselves? What ever will we do?" I said, meeting his eyes. Brent kissed me the way he always did now. Body and soul, so deeply, so passionately I didn't know whether to laugh or weep. All I knew was that it was perfection. And it was mine.

The End